THE SPIRIT FLYER SERIES

THE PERFECT STAR

Becoming Children of the True King

JOHN BIBEE

Illustrated by Paul Turnbaugh

INTERVARSITY PRESS
DOWNERS GROVE, ILLINOIS 60515

InterVarsity Press is the book-publishing division of InterVarsity Christian Fellowship, a student movement active on campus at hundreds of universities, colleges and schools of nursing in the United States of America, and a member movement of the International Fellowship of Evangelical Students. For information about local and regional activities, write Public Relations Dept., InterVarsity Christian Fellowship, 6400 Schroeder Rd., P.O. Box 7895, Madison, WI 53707-7895.

Cover illustration: Paul Turnbaugh

ISBN 0-8308-1206-7

Printed in the United States of America ∞

Library of Congress Cataloging-in-Publication Data
Bibee, John.
    The perfect star/by John Bibee; illustrated by Paul Turnbaugh.
        p.   cm.—(The Spirit Flyer series; 7)
    Summary: The children who ride the Spirit Flyer bikes and serve the Three Kings try to save Tiffany Favor, as their struggle against ORDER and the sinister Goliath Industries approaches its climax.
    ISBN 0-8308-1206-7
    [1. Fantasy.]   I. Turnbaugh, Paul, ill.   II. Title.   III. Series.
PZ7.B471464Pe   1992
[Fic]—dc20

                                                                        92-5686
                                                                        CIP
                                                                        AC

15	14	13	12	11	10	9	8	7	6	5	4	3	2	1
04	03	02	01	00	99	98	97	96	95	94	93	92		

*For the John William
and Celesta Elizabeth Kramar clan,
who are too many to mention,
but especially:*

*Grandma Lois Kramar
and Aunt Thelma Kramar
Glenn and Jan Kramar who begat:
Ellen
Doris
Lucinda (whom I married)
Lois
Julie
Rebecca
John
Stephen*

*You all showed me
the love of the Kings!*

MAKING A
MOVIE IN
CENTERVILLE
• • • • • • • •

1

Some children seem to have almost everything, yet something is still missing, like pieces gone from a giant puzzle. They have a nice home, all the right toys, and even lots of friends. But when everything is counted, when all the points are added up and all the friends assembled, they still have a hunger or thirst for something more. Deep inside, they know life would be perfect if they only had this missing piece of the puzzle. But you have to journey into the Deeper World to finish the puzzle, to come face to face with the One who can tell you who you are, the one who can explain and complete the picture . . .

Tiffany Favor was right in the middle of lying to her mother when she looked outside the window and saw the star hanging in the sky. For some reason it reminded her of some mysterious Christmas ornament hanging all by itself. Looking at the distant star, she shivered and felt uneasy. She stopped talking. Her mother waited.

"Well, did you finish practicing or not, young lady?"

"I . . . uh, " Tiffany stammered. The star hung there silently, as if listening, as if waiting for the answer. "I . . . uh, almost finished. Just five more minutes."

"Good . . . ," her mother said without enthusiasm. Tiffany could tell that her mother wasn't satisfied. But so what else was new, the girl thought. She was never satisfied. But she did believe the lie that there were only five minutes left, when actually Tiffany still had twenty-five to do. Tiffany was glad her mother bought the lie.

"Just make sure you get those five minutes in," her mom said. "We only want you to fulfill your potential, darling. Someday you'll thank your father and me for pushing you to be your best. Now get on with it. Remember, I'll be listening."

"What do you think the star is going to do?" Tiffany asked.

"What?" Mrs. Favor replied. "Are you even listening to me?"

Her mom looked out the window. When she saw the star, she looked almost angry. She shook her head from side to side.

"It's just some harmless comet or asteroid or something," Mrs. Favor said. "It's nothing for you to worry your pretty little head about. I declare, everyone is making such a fuss about some silly light in the sky. ORDER scientists have everything under control. Let them worry about it. Now back to practice. Practice makes perfect, as they say. You should practice in the morning like Sloan and get it out of the way if you don't enjoy it. He does his scales and pieces and he's done."

"I'm not Sloan!" Tiffany snapped.

"Don't be tart with me, young lady," her mother replied, "or we'll start removing privileges again. Do you want that?"

"No," Tiffany said softly, trying to control her temper. She had just gotten done with three weeks of restrictions two days ago. Tiffany knew she was already teetering on the edge of more discipline because of a poor performance on her last report card.

"Your brother is just smart about how he approaches life. That's all I'm saying," Mrs. Favor continued. "And I would think you would want to be the same way. Do you hear me?"

"Yes, Mother," Tiffany said. "But what's the point of practicing? I'm never going to be a concert pianist. Besides, they say that star might run right into the earth and destroy it, destroy us all. What's the point if we're all going to be blown up anyway?"

"That's a bunch of nonsense," Barbie Favor said shrilly to her daughter. Tiffany was surprised at the tone of her mother's voice. For a moment her mother really looked uncertain, and Mrs. Favor usually made a habit of not being uncertain about anything. Deep inside, Tiffany felt fear tugging at her own heart. "Now, I want you to ignore these lies those Rank Blank people are spreading and practice. You have a recital coming up. You can be the star pupil, if you'll just practice."

"Yes, Mother," Tiffany said. Mrs. Favor smiled uneasily, and then left the room. Tiffany let out a deep breath. She looked back at the star, which hadn't seemed to have changed at all. It was hard to believe it was moving toward the earth at such a rapid speed, as the scientists had said. When you looked at it, it didn't seem to move at all. Yet deep in her heart, she knew it was getting closer. Like everyone else in the world, she wondered what was going to happen.

Apparently, scientists had known about the star for some time because they had seen it in their telescopes. It was only in the last few months that you could really see it in the sky without a telescope. Each day it seemed a little bigger as it got closer. There were rumors that the star would crash into the earth and cause a huge disaster like no one had ever seen before. She looked out the window at the star once again. A growing fog seemed to be coming in as the sky began to cloud up.

"Don't worry my silly little head," Tiffany sniffed. "That star could affect everyone's life and future. And she acts like it's nothing or like I don't understand. What do they think I am, some stupid doll? Mom still treats me like a baby."

Tiffany looked around her room. Her bed and dresser and every other object in the room was covered with dolls and a menagerie of stuffed animals. She had so many that her father had put shelves on the walls. Tiffany was proud of her collection of silent, colorful friends. A big tiger was sleeping on her bed next to an adorable bear. The expensive, dressy dolls were on the shelves. They were more to look at than play with or cuddle. She went to the bed and lay down by Tigeroo, the name she had given the tiger several years ago. She hugged the orange and black tiger, but its fake fur didn't immediately make her feel better like it used to. She sat up and threw the animal down.

Looking at the dolls and stuffed animals that morning made her feel weary somehow. Now they seemed like so much junk, cluttering everything up.

"I ought to just throw them all out in the trash," Tiffany said angrily. She took a deep breath.

"I can't hear you!" her mother shouted up the stairs. Tiffany frowned and sat down in front of her keyboard. She turned up the volume and attacked the keys. A terrible noise erupted from the instrument.

"I hope she heard that," Tiffany muttered. She started playing the scales, up and down, up and down, trying to play out some of her impatience and anger. She played faster and made mistakes. She felt terrible when she made mistakes. Mistakes were such messes.

"You're playing too fast!" her mother called up the stairs. "It's not a race."

"It's no fun either," Tiffany said to herself. But she slowed down, making sure to check her watch. "Four minutes and fifty-seven seconds more to go. But what's the point? I thought the summer was going to be more fun than this." She played the scales, but her mind wasn't on

the music. "I don't know why we have to be stuck in this stupid little town. Nothing ever happens here."

The Favor family had moved to Centerville the previous fall in the beginning of her sixth-grade year. Her father, Ken Favor, was executive vice president of the Goliath Factory that had just opened up. He was the most important man in town in many ways, her mother always said. They lived in the biggest, nicest house in Centerville in an area called Buckingham Estates. They had the biggest private swimming pool in town, a tennis court, a place to play basketball and a big brick barbecue pit to cook outside. Everyone in town wanted to be invited to the parties that Ken and Barbie Favor gave at least once a month.

Tiffany and Sloan had immediately been two of the most popular kids in Centerville, and for sure, the most popular in their classes. They were good at sports and looked perfectly beautiful and handsome. Both had blond hair, beautiful teeth and wonderful smiles. Lots of people said they looked like models in advertisements. They usually got the best grades. Until this year, Tiffany had always had straight A's. But during the last quarter of sixth grade, something changed and she got some B's for the first time in her life. Sloan continued with his perfect record, however. Her mother had almost hit the roof when she saw Tiffany's report card. She was already talking about tutors and extra programs during the summer break to "get Tiffany back up to speed," as she said. "You kids are leaders," her mother had said. "We can't have you falling down on the job. If you have trouble with sixth-grade math, I hate to think what will happen in seventh grade." Tiffany had kept silent. When her mother was in a bad mood, it was no use arguing.

"What a way to start the summer," Tiffany muttered. Summer was a time to have fun. Besides everything else, they were talking about starting year-round school in the middle of July, which was only a month away.

Tiffany mechanically played the scales, not looking at the music. She stared into the mirror above her gold and white dresser. Twenty-six light bulbs surrounded the gold-framed mirror. When they were turned on, Tiffany could see every pore in her lovely face. All her friends said Tiffany was beautiful. But Tiffany never thought so. Every time she looked into the mirror she saw the flaws. She knew she wasn't plain looking, like a lot of girls in town. But she couldn't really believe she was beautiful or special like everyone told her she was. Her blond hair was starting to get too frizzy and unmanageable.

What was worse was her weight. It was plain to see she was too fat. She wasn't fat fat, but she was definitely heavier. For the first time in her life her mother had been telling her not to eat so much. She had even suggested that Tiffany swim laps in the pool to "get better muscle tone for your summer swimming suit." Tiffany knew her mother was talking about being fat, not muscle tone.

"Everyone is always telling you what you are or what you should do or think," Tiffany said. "What do they know?"

In the mirror she saw a mild red bump on her chin. Tiffany just knew it would be a pimple. And she dreaded it. She was at the age to get skin blemishes. She had read a million magazine articles about it. She knew that any morning she was going to wake up with a face full of sores and blisters that would make her look like some adolescent freak. Everyone would call her pizza face and laugh and talk behind her back. So far she had been lucky, but she stared at the red spot with great concern and suspicion.

"Don't frown or squint," Tiffany repeated to herself. Her mother told her that so often it was like a record. "You'll get permanent unhappy lines, and you'll look unhappy and be unhappy and that would be bad. Young girls like you are supposed to be happy all the time, period."

But it seemed harder and harder to be happy for some reason. Things hadn't been working out the way she wanted since she'd moved to Centerville. She had plenty of money points and popularity points. Sloan had been #1 and she had been #2 for months in a row on the Point System. Her parents told her and Sloan that they were like the prince and princess of Centerville. Neither child had wanted to move from the city they used to live in. But the job was a good promotion for Mr. Favor. And they had fit right in. As her father liked to say, she and Sloan were "big fish in a little pond." Tiffany hated the expression.

"Who wants to be a big fish or a little fish or a fish at all?" Tiffany thought to herself. "What's the point?" Tiffany hit the keys harder. The notes went up and down, up and down. It all seemed so mindless and useless.

She wasn't sure when she had stopped feeling like a princess. Sometime after the New Year, after the War Vacation when they were back in school. Something just changed. Tiffany woke up morning after morning, and she just wasn't that happy anymore. Her mother seemed more critical than ever, and her father was busier with his work. Tiffany wasn't sure what had happened. Granny Smith, her most favorite person in the whole world, said she was just growing up.

Maybe it started when her friend Rosemary had gotten sick. Later they found out it was cancer, and Rosemary was now very sick and in the hospital. Though Rosemary hadn't been Tiffany's best friend, her illness was still a great concern to her. She didn't really have a best friend, unless it was Granny Smith.

When the Favors moved to Centerville, Tiffany's great aunt had moved to a retirement home nearby so they could be together. Even though she wasn't really their grandmother, Tiffany and the family always called her Granny Smith because she was so special. Tiffany went to visit her every week or so, and sometimes Granny Smith would come for a meal at their house. But as close as they were, Granny didn't seem exactly like a friend, since she was a relative.

Tiffany had friends, but she didn't really trust them deep down. All the kids she knew acted friendly to others when they were around, but as soon as they walked away, they began talking about each other in mean ways, putting each other down. Tiffany was sure they said the same kind of mean things about her behind her back.

Tiffany had also fallen in love, or she thought she was in love with an eighth-grade boy named Zack Peterson, Rosemary's older brother. But Zack treated her like his younger sister. He didn't seem remotely interested in her as a girlfriend. He wasn't that handsome. He was quiet and studious. But he was nice to Tiffany, and she never heard him say mean things about his friends or other kids. That alone made him seem special. But what made him even more special was that he seemed out of reach, and not really interested in her. She knew lots of boys would like to have her as a girlfriend, but not Zack.

As she was thinking about Zack, her brother Sloan came bounding up the stairs, acting as though he were in a hurry. Sloan was always were in a hurry. Her brother was a year older, and Tiffany felt doomed to follow him through life. He was always a little better in school and sports and other activities. He could even play the keyboard better than Tiffany. Everything seemed to come easy to Sloan. Moving to Centerville hadn't seemed to bother him, yet Tiffany wondered about her brother.

Sloan had been different ever since last Halloween when a game they were playing out at a place called Bicycle Hills had gotten out of hand. For several weeks after Halloween, Sloan had been pale and sick, and none of the doctors had known what was the matter. For one whole week he had been burning up with a terrible fever. But because of the Halloween War, as people called it, there were other things to worry about.

Sloan had always been confident and sure of himself before, but after his long sickness he had changed. The confidence and certainty were still there, but now there was a hardness in him, a kind of meanness that hadn't been there before.

He wasn't nearly as much fun to be around because he had gotten even bossier. He was head of the most admired Commando Patrol in town, and he acted like he was a little general preparing to run everyone's life.

Mary Ann called just as Tiffany was counting down the last thirty seconds of her practice. Tiffany answered the phone in her room. Both she and Sloan had their own phone lines.

"You've got to go see it now!" Mary Ann practically yelled into the phone.

"See what?" Tiffany asked.

"Well, I'm not sure what to call it," Mary Ann said. "But it's happening this afternoon. And it's the greatest thing that's ever happened in Centerville. Everyone is saying so."

"But what is it?" Tiffany asked.

"Some kind of movie star thing," Mary Ann replied breathlessly.

"Movie stars are here in Centerville?" Tiffany asked. For once it sounded like something exciting would happen in Centerville.

"No, not here, at least not now," Mary Ann said. "But they're looking for movie stars. They want to make a movie here. We'll all be famous! Just think of it!"

"Slow down," Tiffany said.

"I can't. I'll be right over on my bike. See ya," Mary Ann said and hung up before Tiffany could ask another question. Tiffany wondered whether Mary Ann was telling the truth. Mary Ann was a popular girl in the group of kids that Tiffany more or less led. But Mary Ann was sometimes too flighty and tended to exaggerate things.

Tiffany checked her face in the mirror and brushed her hair, then sprayed it extra long on the part that was curling up too much.

"Stay down," she commanded her hair. Then she ran downstairs.

"I'm going bike riding with Mary Ann," Tiffany yelled to her mother. Mrs. Favor was in her jogging outfit. Her mom was as thin as a broomstick. The doctors had done a body fat analysis and said she was in perfect proportion of body fat to overall weight. Her mom wanted Tiffany to get the same analysis, but Tiffany kept delaying the appointment. She knew the proportions would be wrong, which would mean her mom would put her on some exercise program for sure. She already had to do gymnastics three times a week for the summer.

"You're still having problems with your hair, aren't you?" Mrs. Favor said. She was doing stretching exercises, warming up.

"I've done everything I know how," Tiffany whined. "It just won't stay down."

"Maybe I can have Marcel, my new hairdresser in Kirksville, look at it," Mrs. Favor said. "Everyone says he's very good."

"Well, I'm just going on a bike ride with Mary Ann," Tiffany said.

"But you're still a leader and a trend setter in this town," Mrs. Favor said. "Don't forget it."

"I'm sure I won't," Tiffany muttered as she quickly left the room. At least her mom didn't say anything else about practicing her music. Tiffany got her bike from the garage and rolled it outside. She put her purse on the handlebars.

She had a golden Goliath Super Wings. Everything was shiny and clean. Her parents made sure she and Sloan kept their bikes in good shape. It was part of their chores. Besides their rooms, their homework, and other chores, their bicycles also got inspected twice a week.

Mary Ann shouted from down the street. Tiffany hopped on her bike and coasted down the driveway. They met halfway down the block. Mary Ann was a little red in the face.

"Gosh, Mary Ann, you're almost sweating!" Tiffany said.

"Oh no, really?" Mary Ann asked. Her bright purple purse, a Bike Bag brand, was looped over the handlebars just like Tiffany's. She got a small mirror out of the bag and checked her face. "We'll have to ride slower, but I had to get here as fast as I could," Mary Ann said. "We want to be the first in line over at this Professor Pickie's place."

"Professor who?" Tiffany asked.

"Professor Pickie," Mary Ann said. "At least that's what the poster said."

"What poster?"

"I don't have time to explain."

Just then, Sloan came shooting out of the garage on his Goliath Super

Wings bike. His gray ORDER Commando uniform looked fresh and snappy.

"Where are you going?" Tiffany asked.

"Down to the community center like you and everyone else," Sloan said as if he were bored. "They say they're going to make a movie in Centerville and use kids who live here as the stars. Of course, that means they'll want me."

Sloan sped off. The two girls were close behind.

THE MARK
OF
PERFECTION
· · · · · · · ·

2

Tiffany and Mary Ann rode side by side down the streets of Centerville. The little town seemed prettier in the summer, Tiffany thought. Large green trees were in most yards. The streets were very clean, especially since ORDER Commando Patrols had begun to keep litter picked up. The community center was on the northeast side of town, and Buckingham Estates was in the south part. That day there was a chill in the air because of the increasing clouds and fog.

"We don't have to be in such a rush," Tiffany said, slowing her bike down. Mary Ann slowed down too. "I'm tired of rushing off after Sloan all the time, following him around, doing what he does. Besides, if we go too fast, my hair will mess up worse than it already is."

"It is kind of sticking out a little, isn't it?" Mary Ann replied. "Sharon Simpson said it looked like you put your finger in a light socket."

"Did she really say that?" Tiffany demanded. "That rat is always talking behind my back. I don't even know why I let her hang around our group. Her hair is nothing special. I even saw her Point Breakdown sheet one time. She was afraid to let me see it, but I took it out of her purse when she went to the office. She had negative points under Hair. I can't believe she's criticizing mine. Her hair looks like stuffing out of an old mattress."

"A regular rat's nest," Mary Ann added. Both girls laughed. They rode north on Main Street. They passed the toy store and rode into the town square. The old county courthouse stood in the center of the square. The building was made of huge white stone blocks, a monument to law and order. Now the building's official new title was Point Central of District 66, Cell 17. The government had hung a gigantic Big Board just below the dome a few months before on Number Day.

"Let's check the Point Central Big Board," Tiffany said. "Maybe it's working. I don't like it when the Point System is on the blink."

"At least we can still buy things," Mary Ann said. "I got a new blouse last night."

"Really? You'll have to show it to me later," Tiffany said.

The girls pedaled over to the front of the old courthouse. The long black Big Board hung clear across the front of the old building. The large black panel was over fifty feet long and over thirty feet high. The sight of it always made Tiffany shiver. It seemed so powerful and mysterious and dark, even when lit up with information.

****

BIG BOARD - POINT CENTRAL OF District 66, Cell 17
POINT SYSTEM PLUS ON LINE!!!
POINT SYSTEM PLUS—Rank Categories: Technical Difficulties.
Please Stand By . . .
****

"The Ranking system is still messed up!" Tiffany moaned. "Why can't they fix it? Nobody knows where they stand anymore. It hasn't been this bad since the war last fall. What's your number card look like?"

Mary Ann pulled a small black plastic card out of her pocket. The number card was two inches wide and three inches long. A shadowy, dark picture of Mary Ann's face was embedded into the card. On one side of the card it said RANK. Normally numbers would appear there to show the person's rank, but since the local Point System wasn't working correctly, the space was empty.

Tiffany took out her number card. Her card looked exactly like Mary Ann's card, except it contained a tiny portrait of Tiffany. Tiffany stared down at the blank space where her Rank should have been listed.

"You and Sloan must still be on top," Mary Ann said. "Everyone says so. You guys are always first and second."

"I know," Tiffany said slowly, "but I'd still like to know it *officially*. It's driving my mother nuts too. She gets real nervous when she doesn't know where we stand."

"I don't see how they can let it go on and on like it has," Mary said, nodding. "It's too important to be malfunctioning."

"At least the Wealth Tracker is working," Tiffany said. "That's on the worldwide network. My father says that it is impossible for that part of the system to fail since they have so many backups and emergency measures to keep it working."

"I just wish they'd get the other parts of the system going," Mary Ann said. "Do you think it's true what they say about that star having some kind of effect on the Point System? I saw on the television that several places are having trouble with local Point Systems not working. Some people say the star is causing the trouble with radio frequencies or stuff like that."

"I don't know what to think," Tiffany said. She looked up automatically into the sky. "My parents act like it's nothing, but I think they're worried. "

"Even your dad?" Mary Ann asked.

"He says he's not, but I heard him talking to my mother one night when they thought I was in the other room, and he said no one knows for sure what is going to happen with that star. He sounded scared to me. But when I asked him later, he just acted like I was being a silly kid."

"Did he say it was causing the Point System to mess up?" Mary Ann asked.

"He just said the Point System was complicated and too hard to explain," Tiffany said.

"I know I don't understand how it works," Mary Ann said. She stared at the big black panel with respect.

The Point System was a mystery to a lot of people, but no one could deny its importance. The Point System was the reason Big Boards and number cards existed. Everything about a person or a group or a business was broken down into points. The Big Boards, which were all on a network together, kept track of those points for the Point System. For Tiffany the Point System had seemed kind of like a report card at first, only much bigger. The Big Board not only kept track of students' grades and scores on tests, but it also kept track of everything else you could imagine—from I.Q. points to athletics points to good and bad points to overall personality points and popularity points. Then those points, negative and positive, were all added up to form a person's overall point total or score. The higher your overall point number, the better your rank. And the better your rank, the more everyone thought of you.

That year, the Point System had expanded and grown to cover more and more of life. All businesses, schools and government offices used Big Boards. Even the town library had shifted over. Because the Point System was so effective, the ORDER government had even switched the economic system over to the new Point System Plus on a historic day in April called Number Day.

On Number Day, Centerville and the whole country and every other country in the world had agreed with ORDER's plan to stop using cash money. Ever since then, a person needed a number card to buy or sell anything. The ORDER government figured this would cut down on crime and people cheating each other, since those things usually involved cash. All a person's wealth was converted from dollars to Point System Units. The prices looked the same more or less. For instance, a good pair of tennis shoes cost *75.00, or seventy-five U, as people would say. Everything was kept track of by the new Point System Plus. This new expanded Point System went all around the world. All currencies all over the world had been converted to the Point System Plus by Number Day. There were no more dollars or pounds or marks or yen or rubles. Now there were only PS Units. This made everything more orderly and easy to keep track of, the government insisted. Bankers had much less paperwork to worry about since there were no checks to bother with either. Each person with a valid number card got a monthly or weekly printout of credits and debits. Everything ran smoothly, as long as the Point System Plus remained on line.

But in the last few weeks, several local Point Systems were running into problems, like the one in Centerville. The only part of the systems to have been in trouble were the Ranking numbers. No one had lost any wealth units so far, but they were worried what would happen if the system really broke down. It was bad enough not to have the Ranking part of the system working. Tiffany and many others felt very uneasy not knowing where they stood. Some children checked their rank several times a day, and they just felt lost and out of place when the system wasn't working.

Several other kids were riding their bikes through the square, north on Main Street. They looked excited.

"I bet they're going to the community center too," Mary Ann said. "We better get over there before we miss something."

"I guess," Tiffany said. She was now satisfied that she wasn't just following Sloan like an obedient puppy.

The two girls rode quickly. When they arrived, Tiffany was surprised at the crowd already gathered in the community center parking lot. She saw several children that she knew. As they zipped into the lot, she saw another crowd of children gathering too. But these kids were all riding red Spirit Flyer bicycles. Tiffany knew a lot of them—the Kramar kids, Daniel Bayley and Amy Burke. She saw Josh Smedlowe and his cousin Barry in the middle of the group. Josh was talking and pointing at the truck. A boy named Roger Darrow was standing on the outside of the group. He seemed to be without a bicycle.

"What are those Rank Blank idiots doing around here?" Mary Ann asked.

"I don't know," Tiffany said. She looked at Josh. As she stared at him, he looked across the parking lot straight at her. Tiffany felt embarrassed to be caught staring. Josh waved and began pedaling her way.

"Oh, no," Tiffany said. "Josh Smedlowe is coming over here."

"Good-by," Mary Ann said and hurriedly pedaled away. Tiffany was tempted to follow, but something made her wait.

"Hi, Tiffany," Josh said. Susan Kramar had come over with him. "I felt like I had to talk to you."

"I'm really kind of busy," Tiffany said.

"I just want to say you can't ride the bikes, if they offer them to you," Josh said seriously. "If they offer you a chance to ride a bike with a black box on the handlebars, don't do it."

"What are you talking about?" Tiffany asked. "This is about a movie Goliath is making. I think you've been out in the sun too long. Good-by."

Tiffany turned and pedaled after Mary Ann, relieved to be free of talking to Josh. Being around Rank Blank Spirit Flyer kids made her uneasy. It could even hurt your Point System ranking if you didn't watch out.

Tiffany hopped off her bike. She leaned it against an oak tree. She ran over to the gathering crowd of children standing in front of a long black tractor-trailer truck. A banner hung on the side of the truck.

****

GOLIATH SUPERSTAR CONTEST!!!
BE A STAR IN THE FIRST CENTERVILLE MOVIE!!!
AUDITIONS BEGIN MONDAY, JUNE 15TH!!!

****

Tiffany pushed her way through the crowd to the front where Mary
Ann, Sharon and the other girls in her group of friends were standing.
A freshly built wooden stage stood in front of the trailer. Two large
movie cameras and two big floodlights were on each end of the stage.
A row of metal folding chairs was lined up along the back. In the center
of the stage was a tall microphone stand.

Sloan Favor was in the middle of a group of boys in gray uniforms.
He was talking fast and occasionally pointing over to the group of Spirit
Flyer kids watching from a distance.

Just then, a black Jeep with a red light on top pulled into the parking
lot. On the door were the words "ORDER Security Squad." A tall man
in a gray uniform got out of the Jeep. It was Captain Sharp. A black
limousine rolled into the parking lot beside the Jeep. An old, thin man
got out along with some other men who joined Captain Sharp. One of
the men was Mr. Favor.

"Daddy and Mr. Cutright!" Tiffany said to Mary Ann. "What do they
have to do with this?"

The men walked through the crowd of excited children and climbed
up the steps onto the stage. As they crossed the stage, the big back doors
of the trailer truck opened. A man in a white scientist's coat walked out.
He was a very tall man. He had a thin, very handsome and very tanned
face, with blond-white hair that was long in the back. He walked slowly
and deliberately across the stage and shook hands with Cyrus Cutright.

The man in the white coat walked back inside the trailer. In a moment
he reappeared, pushing two shiny new bicycles with black boxes attached to the handlebars. The children in the crowds started whispering

and pointing when they saw the bicycles. Tiffany frowned, remembering what Josh had said just a few minutes before. But the bicycles had been out of sight then. How could he have known about them, she wondered.

"What kind of bike is that?" Tiffany asked.

"I don't know," Mary Ann replied. "I can see the word 'Goliath.' What's that box?"

"I don't know, but it looks sort of familiar," Tiffany said, her voice rising in excitement.

The old, thin man named Cyrus Cutright stepped up to the microphone. He cleared his throat. Mr. Cutright was the only one higher than Mr. Favor out at the Goliath factory. Something about the old man always gave Tiffany the creeps whenever she was around him, but she never said anything because he was her father's boss. He had small yellow teeth, thin white hair and very wrinkled, leathery skin. Tiffany had once told Sloan that Mr. Cutright looked like he was one hundred years old. Sloan had said he thought one hundred and fifty seemed more like it.

"I'd like to introduce you to one of Centerville's newest and finest citizens," Mr. Cutright began. "This man is a world-class scientist. In recent years he has combined his study with film and video production. He is currently working on one of Goliath's most important projects. Centerville is very lucky indeed to be chosen as one of the experimental sites of this new effort. As many of you have recently become aware, Centerville and its citizens have been chosen to be a part of a major motion picture! Some of you may even star in this important film!"

The children in the audience cheered and clapped. Tiffany nudged Mary Ann in the ribs, smiling. She just knew she would get the starring role for the girl's part.

"To kick off this project, he has a special treat today for you children," the old man said. "May I introduce Professor Prescott P. Pickie."

The children clapped and cheered as the white-haired professor stepped to the front of the stage. His smile seemed extra white and big against his very tanned face.

"I'm so pleased to be welcomed into Centerville," Professor Pickie said. "In a few days, my wife and children will join me as we make Centerville our new home. In the meantime, I want you all to be thinking about auditioning for our feature film to be titled *The Mark of Perfection*."

The children murmured and talked among themselves. Professor Pickie smiled broadly.

"*The Mark of Perfection* is an action-packed film produced by Goliath Industries to help promote one of our most important scientific advances of the century," the professor said. "And to find the right talent for this very important, fascinating film, we're holding the Goliath Super-Star Contest and Audition, right here in Centerville."

"Yes!" Tiffany said, just as excited as all the other kids around her. The children all crowded closer to the stage.

"We'll be looking for a Number One boy and girl as our stars," Professor Pickie said. "But there will be plenty of room for supporting players too. I just know we can find all the talent we need right here in Centerville."

The children cheered again and clapped. They looked at each other excitedly. Nothing like this had ever happened in the small town of Centerville before.

"To help kick off this occasion, we want to show you what else you can look forward to," Professor Pickie said. He pulled the microphone from the stand and, holding it, walked slowly over to one of the shiny new bicycles. He patted the sleek seat of the bicycle. "This is the first of a new concept in a whole new age of bicycle and transportation design. To help celebrate some recent scientific discoveries and processes, Goliath has developed a brand new bike that will make every other bicycle ever made obsolete. I want to introduce to you the Goliath UltraFlight."

The children surged forward to get a better look. Even those in the back of the crowd, Josh Smedlowe and the other kids, were watching with interest. The gold and black bicycle had a unique wide middle bar with a white circle with a white X inside. Shiny golden letters on the black background spelled out the words *Goliath UltraFlight.*

"To show you what this bicycle can do, I need a volunteer, someone ranked in the top ten in the Point System," Professor Pickie said.

A groan went up in the crowd. The children looked at each other in confusion. Professor Pickie seemed surprised, and then he smiled.

"I forgot there are some temporary technical difficulties with the system here in town," he said. "Who was ranked first when the system was last working?"

"Sloan Favor," voices shouted out. Sloan Favor hopped quickly onto the stage. He smiled his handsome smile and strode over to Professor Pickie.

"I've heard a lot about you, young man," Professor Pickie said with a big smile. He looked out at the crowd of children. "I believe I know your father. Who was next in rank in the Point System?"

"Tiffany Favor," voices shouted out.

Tiffany smiled and shook her head in pleasure. Her blond hair glistened in the light.

"Come on up, Tiffany," Professor Pickie said.

Tiffany ran around to the steps on the side of the stage. She quickly joined her brother. She smiled at her friends watching enviously below.

"You kids look like SuperStar material for sure," Professor Pickie said with a smile. "Now it's time you took the first rides on these Goliath UltraFlight bicycles as we kick off a new age in Centerville's history. Let the rides begin!"

THE RIDE
OF YOUR
LIFE
· · · · · · · · ·

3

Tiffany and Sloan Favor stood on the edge of a new adventure. Professor Pickie took them by the arms and guided them over to the Goliath UltraFlight bicycles.

"You kids are in for the ride of your life," Professor Pickie said. "These UltraFlights are Goliath's newest invention. They work like a regular bike with eighteen internal gears. But their quality goes much deeper than that. All UltraFlights are equipped with a unique invention: the TRAG-Ultra7."

Professor Pickie patted the small black box attached to the center of the handlebars. A crystal lever stuck out of the side of the box.

"The TRAG-Ultra7 is your door to adventure and excitement," Professor Pickie explained. "With the TRAG-Ultra7, we've built a better mousetrap, as they say. Every kid in the world will be riding these bikes once they are Number Marked and become available. With the Goliath Ultra-Flight bikes, you can conquer your dreams, you can conquer all your desires, harnessing the power to be the best you can be. These bikes are made so people can reach their highest heights and control their own destinies like never before. Only you will know the potential you can reach with your Goliath UltraFlight."

Tiffany licked her lips with excitement as she stared at the sleek bicycle. Sloan rested his hand on the smooth metal frame.

"Many of you have heard rumors about other bicycles, I'm sure, ridden by those people who have been against progress and against the peace and safety ORDER has brought all around the world this year. These rebellious individuals, scattered here and there, have made wild and extravagant claims about some very old and very ugly bicycles."

"He's talking about Spirit Flyer bikes," Mary Ann said to Judy.

"Yeah, they're the ugliest bikes I've ever seen," Judy replied.

"In this new age of peace and safety and prosperity, we in Goliath Industries wanted to clear away the smoke about these lies," Professor Pickie said. "We want to show you and children all over the world the difference between the true thing and false imitations. The real thing, my friends, is here before your eyes. The Goliath UltraFlight."

The children in the crowd cheered once more. Some looked to the rear of the crowd at the group of kids sitting on their Spirit Flyer bicycles. Tiffany looked at Josh. He sat up very straight on his bicycle. He seemed to be frowning, though it was hard to tell since he was so far away.

"Hop on, SuperStars," Professor Pickie said. "Let's start the ride of your life. Let the Goliath UltraFlight take you away."

Both Tiffany and Sloan got on the bikes. Out in the crowd, Tiffany saw all the other children look on with envy. She smiled her perfect smile. But in the back of the crowd she saw Josh Smedlowe. He was shaking his head as if telling her not to do it.

"What does he or any of those Rank Blank idiots know?" she thought to herself.

"Like all special machines with unique powers, the UltraFlight requires its own special energy formula, which I just happen to have with me," the professor said. He reached into a big pocket on his white coat and pulled out two sealed glass test tubes. A small label was stuck to each one which said *Wildbird Energy Drops.*

"Wildbird?" Tiffany wondered. The professor walked over and placed a glass tube on top of each of the black TRAG-Ultra7 boxes. The glass tubes lay there for two seconds, and then were instantly sucked deep into the black box. Tiffany flinched because she was so startled.

"The Goliath UltraFlights are fueled for take-off," Professor Pickie said. "Put your number card in the slot on the side of the TRAG-Ultra7."

Both children did as they were told. The strange black box began to hum softly. Sloan smiled.

"Now place your right hand on top of the TRAG-Ultra7," Professor Pickie said. Both children did as they were told. Everyone watched with great interest.

"Ouch!" Tiffany said as the little box clicked. She pulled her hand away. In the middle of her palm was a small red spot—blood. Sloan lifted his hand away too. He looked at a drop of blood. Tiffany stared down at the box. She hadn't seen it before, but there was a very small hole in the middle of the black box.

"That thing stuck me," Tiffany said. "It made me bleed."

"Just a formality," Professor Pickie said softly away from the microphone. He winked at the two children. "It's nothing to worry about. The box is just identifying you with your number card."

"But why does it need . . ."

"You are now ready to begin the ride of a lifetime," the professor announced into the microphone. "Put your right hand on the UltraFlight gear lever."

Sloan and Tiffany each put a right hand on the crystal lever coming out of the box. The kids in the crowd shouted. For a moment, Tiffany felt once again, that she was a princess and Sloan was a prince in their own little kingdom of Centerville. The pain and the drop of blood in her hand were almost forgotten.

"Now for the fun part," Professor Pickie said. "I want you to start pedaling for the edge of the stage. And as you pedal, push the UltraFlight gear lever forward."

"But won't we crash?" Tiffany asked anxiously. The stage was at least three and a half feet off the ground.

"Don't be afraid," the professor said. "Now's the time to look forward."

"I'm not afraid," Sloan announced loudly. He began to pedal the sleek black and gold bicycle. As it moved across the stage, he pushed the crystal lever. The bike jerked and jumped. As he reached the edge of the stage, the thin tires lifted up off the wooden platform. Sloan pedaled faster and pushed the lever farther forward. To everyone's amazement, the bicycle rose up into the air.

There was silence as Sloan just kept going higher and higher. The children stared with open mouths. Sloan wobbled from side to side, but the bike kept going upward. The crowd exploded into a cheer. Sloan looked down.

"I'm flying!" he yelled in glee. "At last I'm really flying!"

He pedaled faster. The bicycle moved a little faster. But as he moved faster, it wobbled and vibrated more and more.

Like the rest of the children, Tiffany stared at Sloan with surprise and wonder. Her hand shook with excitement.

"It's time to follow your brother, Miss SuperStar," the professor said with a smile. Tiffany nodded her head and smiled even though part of her resented being told to follow Sloan. "I want you and Sloan to circle around a few times, then come back and land so I can give you a few further instructions."

Tiffany nodded, then began to pedal. And as she did, she pushed the UltraFlight lever forward.

The bike seemed to lunge to one side, but rose upward into the air. The children whistled and yelled as Tiffany held on tighter. The bike rose higher and higher into the air as the ground fell away. Taking off felt something like going up quickly on a ferris wheel. But this was so different. There was nothing holding her up. The bike just rose higher. Up ahead she saw Sloan. He was turning the handlebars so the bike circled around. Tiffany was almost afraid to look down, but she forced herself. She felt a little queasy when she saw all the upturned faces staring in wonder. They had to be at least twenty feet below her. She wanted to wave at Mary Ann and her other friends, but was too afraid to let go of the handlebars.

The bike rose higher and higher. Tiffany felt a surge of excitement as she rose as high as the branches of the oak tree in the parking lot. Like Sloan, she turned the handlebars, and the bicycle slowly began to turn in midair. She followed Sloan's invisible path in the sky as he flew back over the stage and then over the community center roof itself. Tiffany pedaled faster and caught up with her brother. Up in the air, she could see more fog blowing in.

"This is the ultimate!" Sloan yelled at his sister. His eyes were wild with excitement. He didn't seem nervous at all. "Can you believe it?"

"We're supposed to make a circle, then go back," Tiffany said. "Professor Pickie has some more instructions to give us."

"I want to go faster!" Sloan shouted, acting as if he hadn't even heard her. His legs pumped harder. The bike sped up, but not nearly as much as the boy liked. Tiffany went a little faster, but noticed that the bicycle wobbled more at the higher speed. Sloan shot on ahead and went higher into the sky.

"Sloan, we're supposed to go back for instructions," Tiffany called. But Sloan wasn't listening. He stood up on the pedals and pushed the lever.

Tiffany quit pedaling and pulled the gear lever back, and the bike dropped suddenly like a falling elevator. She pushed the gear forward to stop the fall and quickly began pedaling. The bicycle leveled off. She aimed it for the stage. She slowed down and pushed the lever down as the children cheered. Professor Pickie reached out and grabbed her as she came by. He held on and the bike stopped. The crowd of children shouted and thundered their applause. Tiffany waved proudly to her friends, but inside she felt a bit queasy and somewhat dizzy.

"Better go get your brother," Professor Pickie said softly. He seemed calm, but Tiffany could hear the concern in his voice. "When the fuel runs out, the bike loses power. The UltraFlight lever will start to blink red. You need to land soon after that."

"I told him to come back, but he just took off," Tiffany said. "Where did he go?"

She looked up in the sky. The fog was thicker now, and Sloan had flown out of sight. "I feel a little sick to my stomach."

"It's nothing but first flight jitters," Professor Pickie said. He reached in his pocket and brought out two glass tubes of *Wildbird Energy Drops.* "Give one to your brother and use one yourself when the light begins to blink red and you'll be ok. Now get going!"

Professor Pickie pushed Tiffany toward the edge of the stage. She began to pedal. She pushed the gear lever forward, and the sleek bicycle once again jerked up into the sky. She held on tight, a wave of fear pulsing through her.

She pushed the gear lever farther and the bike went higher. She pedaled faster. She still couldn't see Sloan. She looked down at the ground. All her friends waved. Tiffany was too scared to wave back. Josh and the other Spirit Flyer kids at the back of the crowd were watching with great interest as Tiffany flew higher. The bike was wobbling worse, but Tiffany pedaled faster, trying to see Sloan.

The wind bringing the fog was blowing harder into her face the higher she got. As she rose above the trees, she could see the town spread out before her, or what was left of it. Half the town was already hidden in the dense fog which was coming in from the south. Far ahead, she thought she saw Sloan. A dark object was moving in the fog.

"I better go get him before he hurts himself," Tiffany said. She pedaled faster, heading into the fog. She looked back and felt a stab of fear when she could barely see the community center, let alone Professor Pickie or the other kids. The fog seemed to be covering everything so quickly now.

Tiffany turned and looked forward. She still saw the dark object in the sky. She pedaled faster, even though the bicycle wobbled more. She took a deep breath and held on tighter. The queasy feeling in her stomach hadn't gone away. If anything, she felt worse.

Out of the corner of her eye she saw them shoot out of the fog. She screamed as five bicycles came speeding into view. Josh and the other kids on the old junky Spirit Flyer bikes were coming straight at her. Tiffany slowed down. She recognized John and Susan Kramar, Daniel Bayley and Amy Burke. Like everyone else, she had heard rumors about the mysterious old red bicycles and had even thought she'd seen one flying once, but she'd assumed it was all just a dream. Besides, everyone who rode a Spirit Flyer bicycle was Rank Blank and a known enemy to ORDER.

"What are you doing here?" Tiffany demanded as Josh pedaled closer.

"You've got to go back," Josh said. "You're in real danger."

"You're crazy," Tiffany said. "And how do you get those bikes to do that? You don't have a TRAG-Ultra7 or anything."

"The kings hold these bikes up," Josh said with a smile.

"Yeah," Susan Kramar said. "What holds your bike up?"

"I . . . uh . . . it's the TRAG-Ultra7, I guess," she said uncertainly.

"But what makes it work?" Josh asked.

"I don't know," Tiffany blurted out. "And I don't care as long as I'm flying. I'm really in a hurry now."

Josh nodded, his face was serious. "I tell you, we saw this all happening several days ago. We knew they would give you bikes that fly. But they're up to no good. You've got to land that thing and never ride it again."

"I've got to go get Sloan," Tiffany said. "Just . . . just . . . leave me alone."

"He's in danger too," Susan Kramar called out to Tiffany. "We wouldn't lie to you. We want to help you."

"Then just leave me alone," Tiffany said, feeling more and more afraid. "I've got to get Sloan some more energy drops, and then we'll return to Professor Pickie, and we'll all be fine. I don't want your . . . help."

She turned and rode forward into the sky. When she didn't hear anything, she looked back. The kids on the Spirit Flyer bicycles had just seem to stop in the sky. Tiffany was surprised they weren't falling. The fog was getting thicker and thicker. She could barely see a shape moving up far ahead. She clenched her teeth and flew faster.

Far ahead in the fog, two red eyes watched the girl on the bicycle coming closer. The eyes began to glow more brightly as she came closer to the open mouth.

Josh Smedlowe and the other children on the old red Spirit Flyer bicycles stood still in the sky and watched the girl pedal off into the distance.

"We've got to stop her!" Amy Burke shouted.

"We tried to warn her," Josh said, shaking his head sadly.

"Everything is coming true just like we saw in our mirrors," John Kramar added. He reached down and touched the mirror attached to his handlebars. "I never thought they would come up with bikes that could fly."

"They're not the same," Susan Kramar said. "Did you see how they shook when they flew? They don't seem very reliable."

"They can't be reliable if they're made by Goliath," Josh said.

"Look out!" Susan suddenly cried out. Right before their eyes, it rose up out of the fog. A snake's head as big as a building was opening its giant mouth wider and wider.

"We better get out of here," Amy Burke said. She began to turn her bike around.

"Wait!" Josh said, staring with fascination. "It's not after us. It's after Tiffany."

The children watched. The giant mouth kept opening more and more as it moved behind Tiffany.

"We've got to help her," Josh said. "Tiffany!"

The children began to shout out across the sky. But Tiffany didn't turn around to see what was behind her. She rode forward and disappeared into the thick fog. The huge serpent was close behind.

Tiffany's skin felt very chilly and cold. She thought she heard some distant voices. Everything seemed be getting darker too.

"Sloan!" she called out. But her voice seemed swallowed up by the fog. Then the darkness suddenly covered her. The bicycle bumped into something and stopped, dead. She couldn't see a thing as she screamed out.

THE PRINCE AND PRINCESS

· · · · · · · ·

4

Tiffany shivered in the damp cold darkness. For the first time in her life, she felt completely alone and isolated. The deep darkness seemed to be not only around her, but inside her body.

"Sloan?" Tiffany said. "Somebody? . . . Anybody here? I must have crash-landed somewhere. But why is it so dark?"

Tiffany was afraid to get off the bike. She sat on the seat and shivered, trying to stop the fear that was growing inside. Then she heard a voice. She turned around. Off in the far distance, she could see a very faint light. Tiffany turned the bike and began to pedal toward the light. She seemed to be in some long black tunnel. She felt in her pocket to make sure the two vials of Wildbird Drops were still there. The light got closer.

The sound of voices got louder. Somehow they seemed familiar. She pedaled faster, trying to escape the dark shadows. As she got closer to the light, the tunnel suddenly turned sharply in a kind of curve in the dark fantasy. As she rounded the turn, everything became extremely bright.

Tiffany blinked in surprise. She was right in front of a beautiful, magnificent castle. The castle looked just like the kind lived in a long time ago by kings and queens. A moat circled the high stone walls. A cobblestone street ran in front of the castle. Down below in the valley, Tiffany saw a distant town. The whole scene was like something out of a movie or a storybook.

Brilliant bright lights were shining behind her, pointing at the castle. Thick black electric cords ran from the lights down another dark hall where there was a sound of motors running. Tiffany looked behind her. The tunnel she had come through no longer seemed to be there, as if it had closed off.

"What's going on?" Tiffany asked. "Did I fall down into some cave or what?"

Then she saw Sloan. He was standing on a drawbridge that led into the castle. He was holding a shining sword in his hand. He waved at Tiffany.

"Tiffany, come down," he shouted. "This place is great!"

Tiffany pedaled the Goliath UltraFlight down toward Sloan. As she got closer, she felt as if she was at the crossroads of some great decision. She pedaled the bicycle across the drawbridge. As she did, a voice yelled out in the darkness, "Ready on the set!"

"What is this place?" Tiffany asked. She got off her bicycle, looking around in wonder. It seemed as if she had crossed over into a whole other world, unlike any other place she had seen. They were in a quaint little countryside scene, with the castle on the top of a hill. The castle seemed huge and powerful. Birds sang in round lollipop trees. Flowers bloomed everywhere. The smell of roses and freshly baked bread was in the air. Down the cobblestone street, the town in the valley below seemed closer now and more real. Off in the distance, rolling hills faded into a purple sky. If you looked in that direction, everything seemed like a fairy-book world, peaceful and happy and secure. But as Tiffany turned around and looked in the direction from which she had come, the fairy-book land and castle all abruptly ended in a line of darkness. On one side it was the wonderful land, and then as suddenly as if turning a page, the land was gone. Above them, there was really no sky at all, only darkness.

"What an odd place," the girl said softly. "How did we get here? I feel like I'm in a storybook place. And why are you dressed in those old clothes?"

"It's like a costume or something," Sloan said. "Or maybe it's just who I am. I don't know how we got here, but I don't want to leave. It seems like I've been here hours. I'm a prince here. And you're the princess. They adore us here."

"A princess? Really?" Tiffany asked. She began to feel pleased.

"Sure," Sloan said. "Look at yourself!"

Tiffany gasped as she looked down. Now she was wearing a very beautiful gown covered with jewels and golden slippers on her feet. A golden crown was on her head. A heavy golden necklace hung around her neck. A large round medallion was attached to the chain. A round circle with an X inside was stamped in the gold on the chain. Sloan was wearing a golden chain and medallion just like his sister's. The medallions look like the sign of royalty, the girl thought proudly. Tiffany touched it. Underneath it, she still saw the tiny chain and locket that Granny Smith had given her. She was bothered a bit by the thought of what Granny Smith might think of all this. She wondered if Granny would approve.

"Lights!" a voice shouted out. "And *action!*"

44

Tiffany whirled around, looking back across the drawbridge. All around them were rows of bright lights shining down on them.

"The lights are so bright I can't see behind them," Tiffany said. "Where are we and what is going on?"

"Get ready!" a voice shouted out. "Prince, you need to get ready for the sword-fight sequence."

"Another sword fight?" Sloan asked. "I already slew a big green dragon. What could be next?"

As if to answer, several ugly slimy creatures crawled up out of the moat, shrieking and gurgling. Tiffany screamed and jumped back as Sloan swung his sword around to face them. The slimy creatures were covered in mud and muck. Though they cried out in loud voices, their lips didn't seem to move, as if they were wearing masks. The faces or masks seemed familiar. Tiffany was surprised that one of the faces looked just like Josh Smedlowe. Then she recognized the others. They were the faces of the Rank Blank kids, the ones who rode Spirit Flyer bicycles.

"I will defeat any rebellion!" Sloan said automatically. He leaped forward and began hacking at the muddy rebels. As he hit each one with his shining blade, great sparks of light sizzled and popped. One by one, the attackers fell back into the murky waters of the moat as they were hit. Two of the creatures came at the same time and knocked away the sword. Sloan appeared to be in danger.

"I will help you, my brother, the Prince," Tiffany heard herself say. She felt as if she was watching herself in a movie as she ran forward, holding up her right hand. A flash of light like a laser shot out of her hand and hit one creature and knocked him off his feet, throwing him backward into the moat. She automatically aimed the light at the other attacker, and he too was knocked backward into the water, a large smoking hole cut clear through him. Both Tiffany and Sloan ran to the edge of the moat just in time to see the muddy waters swallow up the last of the attackers.

"Cut!" a voice called out loudly. Then they heard other voices.

"Hail, Princess Tiffany! Hail, Prince Sloan!" voices shouted out. Coming up the old cobblestone road were children dressed like peasants from long ago. As they got closer, Tiffany recognized their faces—they were the kids from Centerville. Mary Ann was first in line, along with Amanda and Jennifer and Sharon. All the other kids were there too. They were smiling and holding gifts in their hands. They came up one by one and dropped them at Prince Sloan's and Princess Tiffany's feet. Though they looked happy, the town's children also seemed to have stiff, masklike faces, just like the attackers from the moat.

"Hail to the Prince and Princess—The Marks of Perfection!" the children shouted with one voice. Then they all dropped to their knees and bowed low before Sloan and Tiffany. As they raised their heads, they smiled and began to cheer and clap. Tiffany smiled back, nodding her head, as if to show she accepted their praise and adoration.

"You saved us all from the rebel forces!" they yelled. "You saved us all!"

The children continued bowing and clapping. Then the sound increased, all around them. Loud clapping and applause and cheers erupted from behind the bright lights. Tiffany smiled automatically because she felt sure the applause and cheers were for her. The appreciative noise flooded over her and made her feel a warm glow inside. The fear and confusion she had been feeling suddenly were gone. She had never felt so accepted and loved. One child came forward lugging a big leather sack. He laid the sack at Princess Tiffany's feet, then backed away, bowing as he went. Tiffany opened the bag. It was filled with sparkling diamonds and emeralds and rubies. She reached down and scooped up the jewels. She let them fall through her fingers like a waterfall of color. She smiled and then grabbed handfuls of the gems and put them into her pockets.

Tiffany looked down at her right hand. In the center of her palm was a small blue circle with an X in the center.

"Did that light come out of here?" she asked.

"Of course it did, my dear," a man's voice said. Tiffany looked up. Out of the wall of blinding bright lights, a tall man in a white coat walked across the drawbridge. Professor Pickie was smiling his handsome smile.

"Great scene, both of you," the professor said. "I can tell you children are SuperStar material for sure."

"I don't understand what's going on," Tiffany said. She looked at the mark in her hand. "What is this mark in my hand?"

"That's the mark of perfection, of course," Professor Pickie said. "That's the new Number Mark all children shall have on July Fourth. And with it they shall have a Goliath UltraFlight. And with those bicycles, they shall live as princes and princesses in a land free from rebellion and war. The future is grand, my dear, and you definitely have a starring role. Let me congratulate your brother."

Professor Pickie walked over to Sloan. The prince had picked up his shining sword and was wiping goop off the blade. Tiffany still felt confused. She looked at the crowd of children that had come up the cobblestone street. They had not stopped cheering and clapping and bowing down. The expression on their stiff faces was still happy and joyous. They didn't even seem to notice the professor. In fact, the closer Tiffany looked at her friends, the stranger they seemed because they repeated the same cheer and bow over and over again, as if they were robots.

Just then she noticed that the crystal gear lever on her Goliath Ultra-Flight was blinking red. The light on Sloan's bicycle was blinking too.

"Sloan, you need another tube of Wildbird Drops," Tiffany said. Once again she remembered riding in the sky. Tiffany reached and felt where her pocket should have been under her princess costume. The tubes were in there. She pushed a fold of the gown aside and was surprised to see she was wearing her jeans. Earlier, she had really thought she was a princess. But now it seemed more and more as if she had just been a kid playing dress-up. She pulled the vials of red liquid out of her pocket.

"Great scene, great scene," Professor Pickie said. He smiled and walked back across the drawbridge and disappeared into the bright lights.

"You have to put this in your bicycle or else it will fall," Tiffany said.

"Fall?" Sloan said. "You must be crazy. I'm a prince in my kingdom. I'm invincible. Nothing can hurt me."

As he spoke, the crystal levers on the Goliath UltraFlights flashed brighter and more frequently. The drawbridge over the moat began shaking. Sloan and Tiffany backed away from it. With a loud crack, the bridge broke in the middle and fell into the muddy water. The water hissed and steam rose up like smoke.

"I think we better get out of here," Tiffany said. The floor beneath their feet seemed to be trembling.

"Get out of here, and leave my kingdom?" Sloan asked in surprise. "I haven't even begun to explore my domain."

Just then, the door on the castle wall fell forward and crashed right beside them. Tiffany jumped back. She bent over to look at the door. She was shocked to see that the back of the door looked like cardboard with a stick on it. She reached down. The door wasn't heavy at all. She turned it over. It looked just like ancient oak wood, but as she reached down to touch it, she could tell that the wood was really just paint.

"What's going on?" Tiffany asked.

The lights on the bicycles were blinking more and more rapidly. Even Sloan looked concerned. The children on the cobblestone road were running back toward town as the ground shook and the fog began to spread.

"Come back!" Sloan yelled, raising his arm, holding up the sword. As he waved the sword, the sleeve on his beautiful prince's jacket tore. And right before Tiffany's eyes, the rest of his clothes began to shrink and smolder and tear in puffs of smoke. As Sloan whirled and coughed, the smoke grew worse. Tiffany's royal gown seemed to be smoldering too. She hit it, trying to make the smoke stop. Finally, the air cleared. Tiffany stared in surprise at Sloan. All his beautiful royal clothes were now just gray rags.

"Look at your clothes!" Sloan said, pointing at his sister. Tiffany looked down. Instead of the beautiful gown, she was now wearing a heap of gray smoldering rags just like Sloan. She looked back up at him. That's when she saw the chain. Wrapped around Sloan's chest was a heavy dark chain. One end of the chain was connected to a dark ring around Sloan's neck. The other end of the chain ran down into the ground and disappeared into the moat. Tiffany felt for her own royal necklace and medallion. Instead, she touched the cold links of a heavy chain. She looked down and stared at the cold dark links. She felt a sense of dread and disgust fall over her like a blanket as she stared at the chain.

"Let me have those Wildbird Drops," Sloan said. Tiffany gave him a tube. He quickly jumped on his bicycle and placed the tube on top of the black box. With a hiss and a burp, the Wildbird Drops were sucked deep inside the Ultra7. The blinking red crystal lever became clear once again. But the lever on Tiffany's bike was blinking faster. Tiffany ran for her bike. As she got on, Sloan began to pedal away. His UltraFlight left the ground.

"Wait up for me," Tiffany said. She reached out to put her tube of Wildbird Drops on the TRAG-Ultra7 unit. But at that moment, the ground shook violently and she dropped the tube.

"Wait up!" Tiffany yelled. A great groaning sound filled the air, as a piece of the castle wall fell straight toward Tiffany. She backed up, tripping over the bicycle as the wall crashed down. She was sure she would be crushed by the heavy stones as the wall covered her.

But the wall barely even hurt. She stood up and found herself in the middle of a large panel of cardboard with a stick on the back. It was fake, just like the door. The wall was nothing more than paint on cardboard.

The ground was shaking harder now. Tiffany tore through the wall and picked up the bicycle. She searched frantically, ripping through the cardboard for the Wildbird Drops. Something popped beneath her foot. She cried out when she found the tube broken into tiny pieces with all the red liquid spilled out. She looked up. Sloan was almost gone, disappearing into the fog.

"Sloan, come back and help me!" Tiffany screamed. But her brother was gone. The ground shook harder. The water in the moat was sloshing violently up out of the bank as if it were boiling. Smoke filled the air.

Tiffany tried to push her bicycle toward the cobblestone road that led to the little town below. But she could barely move at all because of the heavy chain around her neck.

"Sloan!" she called out in a croaky whisper, her voice choked with deep fear. She scrambled on the bike and tried to pedal, but nothing happened. The light was not blinking anymore now. It was solid red, and almost seemed to be burning.

"Help me!" Tiffany yelled. Another great wall of the castle fell flat. The sky above the castle seemed to be tearing apart like a huge piece of paper. Tiffany stared in terror as the sky itself burst into flames. She called for help, but her voice was drowned out by the destructive roar.

THE CASTLE CRUMBLES

. . . .

5

In the midst of the flaming sky, Tiffany saw a light shining through. The light got brighter and brighter. For a moment she wondered if the star in the sky was coming to crash into her. But then suddenly, a red bicycle shot through the fire. Josh Smedlowe and three others on bikes blazed into the crumbling castleland. Tiffany stared in surprise. Everything was happening too fast. She wasn't sure if she was more surprised to see Josh and the other kids on bikes, or the huge hole in the sky that had ripped open like a big sheet of burning paper. It had seemed so real before. Everything had seemed so real and true and good, and now it was all crumbling.

Josh and the other kids pedaled slowly above the scene, about fifteen feet off the ground. With a flick of his hand, he turned off the light on his old red bicycle and glided down near Tiffany. The big tires of the old bike touched down softly. The other children followed and stopped next to Josh on the trembling surface.

Tiffany jumped back. Josh looked around at the fallen cardboard walls and the boiling water in the moat. John Kramar and Daniel Bayley and Susan Kramar looked at everything in surprise. They then looked at Tiffany and at the chain hanging down her chest.

"We've got to get you out of here," Josh said loudly above the trembling noise.

"But I lost the Wildbird Drops," Tiffany said. "The tube broke."

"What do you mean?" Josh asked. Another castle wall fell with a crash, blowing a huge cloud of fog over the children.

"The UltraFlight won't go without the Wildbird Drops," Tiffany said. "I have to have them. Sloan got his and left. But my tube broke."

"You'll have to come with us then," Josh said. "Hop on my bike."

"No," Tiffany said. "I can't go with you."

"This place is coming apart," Josh said. "And your chain will drag you down."

"What chain? I don't know what you're talking about," Tiffany said, suddenly embarrassed. She wasn't sure why she felt that way, but it seemed most important that no one know about the chain.

"The chain around your neck," the boy replied. "Can't you see it?"

"My Granny Smith gave this to me," Tiffany said, pulling up the chain and locket from around her neck.

"I don't mean that chain," Josh said. "The other one. The one that has you locked up."

"Nothing has me locked up," Tiffany said. As soon as she spoke, the long dark chain began to rattle as the links disappeared into the moat. The chain moved faster and faster, pulling up all the slack. Tiffany watched in surprise and horror as the links clanked as they moved. Then the chained pulled tight, jerking the girl to the ground.

"Sloan!" Tiffany yelled. She was being dragged toward the moat. Josh jumped off the bike. He reached quickly for Tiffany's hand, and she reached out for him, but the chain's pull was quicker. She screamed as she was pulled over the bank of the moat and down into the water. Josh lunged forward. He felt Tiffany's hair as her head went under. He was reaching for her arms. His hand caught on something, but Tiffany was gone. He pulled up his hand and saw the tiny gold chain and locket.

"Use your bike!" Daniel Bayley shouted. Josh nodded silently. He hopped on his Spirit Flyer and turned on the light in one motion. He stood up on the pedals as he headed straight for the moat. The old red bicycle plunged into the water. The light of the Spirit Flyer went before him like a search beam.

Tiffany was being dragged down deeper and deeper into the dark waters. She saw the light of the old bicycle and reached out. Both hands gripped the handlebars. When Josh saw that, he turned the bike. The two children shot upward, following the beam of light. As they flew, Josh suddenly was flanked by Daniel, John Kramar and Susan. Then Amy Burke was beside them too. They cut through the darkness. Tiffany hung onto the handlebars, her eyes closed, trying to block out the fear.

Then the children broke through. They found themselves out of the darkness and just in a dense fog. The bikes slowed down and then softly touched the ground. Tiffany let go of the bike and sat on the ground, which felt very hard. She looked around. She wasn't sitting on the ground at all but on the asphalt road in front of a big new warehouse inside the gates of the Goliath factory. Everything looked familiar and the ground was solid beneath her. A large tractor-trailer truck was pulling away from the gate leading into the factory.

"I think we're safe now," Josh said. "We're back in Centerville anyway."

Tiffany struggled to her feet. She thought her clothes would be soaking wet, but they weren't. She touched her neck. She didn't feel the dark

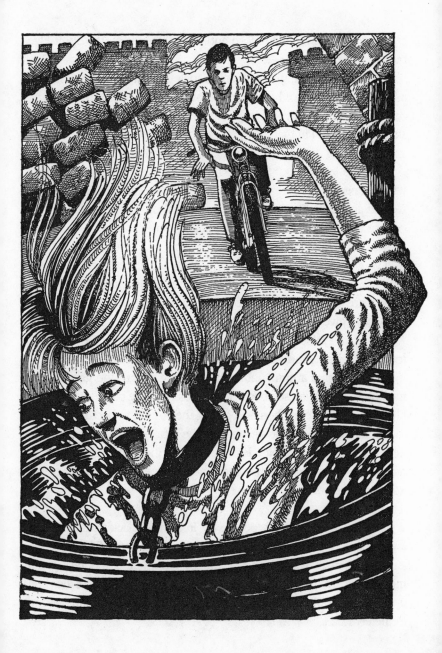

chain either. She looked at Josh and the other kids on the Spirit Flyer bikes with fear in her eyes.

"You guys are trying to pull some trick on me, aren't you?" Tiffany asked accusingly. "I've heard about those Spirit Flyer bicycles."

"We were helping you," Josh said. "Don't you remember? You were sinking fast down in that moat, and we came after you."

"It's all a big trick," Tiffany said, trembling with fear.

"Yes, it is a big trick," Susan Kramar said softly. She stared at Tiffany with concern. "You are being tricked, Tiffany. But it's not by us. It's Goliath and ORDER, and now they're using those new bicycles."

"The UltraFlight!" Tiffany said. "What happened to it?"

"You left it in that place," Josh said. "Don't you remember?"

"I've got to . . . I've got to . . . ," Tiffany looked at each of the five children staring quietly at her, watching her. For a moment she felt as if she were going crazy. "I've got to go home. I've got to go home."

"We can give you a ride," Josh said.

"No-o-o-o!" Tiffany screamed. "Leave me alone. You, all of you are trying to trick me, and I don't like it! And it won't work!"

Tiffany whirled around and began walking toward the gate that led into the factory. Then she began to run. Josh and the other kids on Spirit Flyer bicycles watched her. As a group, they began to pedal toward the big chain-link fence that surrounded the factory grounds. As they got near the fence, all five bicycles rose up into the air, sailed over it and landed on the ground on the other side. They pedaled out to Cemetery Road and waited.

Just inside the gate, two people sat in a small black truck. One was a man dressed in black clothes. He wore a black derby. The other was an old lady with white hair. She looked kind, like someone's grandmother, except for her eyes. She stared at the running girl so hard her eyes almost seemed to glow red. Both of them watched her run out onto Cemetery Road.

"I can't believe I'm stuck with you again," the old woman said with disgust.

"I don't like it any better than you," the man in the derby replied. "A year later and I'm back where I started."

"Get going, you fool, or we'll mess up this assignment too," the woman replied. "I liked you better as a crow. At least you didn't talk so much."

"Well, if you had done your job, we would have had these children and this whole town under control a long time ago," the man replied.

"Oh, shut up and drive," the woman said. "We've got to catch up to that girl."

The black truck pulled out of the parking lot and headed down Cemetery Road. The man lowered his head, hiding his face as he passed Josh and the other children on the Spirit Flyer bicycles.

"Confound those brats!" the man said softly.

"Be quiet or they'll hear you," the woman replied. "I'd like to get my claws into that girl as much as anyone."

The children on the road didn't say anything as Tiffany ran past them. She didn't look at their faces. A few seconds later, the black truck drove by, following Tiffany down the road.

"Hey!" John Kramar said. "Did you see that truck?"

"What about it?" Josh asked.

"It seems real familiar," John said.

"So did the driver," Susan said softly, staring after the truck. "I could have sworn that man looked just like Horace Grinsby."

"All I saw was the derby," John said.

"Grinsby who?" Josh asked.

"He came around Centerville just about a year ago," John said. "We can fill you in later. He works for Goliath. And if he's here, he's up to no good. Maybe we should follow them."

John Kramar turned his bicycle toward town. He immediately began to pedal but then stopped almost as quickly.

"You know, maybe we should wait and ask the kings if we should follow them or not," John said meekly. "I mean, maybe that is Grinsby, but maybe this isn't the time or place to go after him."

"John Kramar, you are learning," Susan Kramar said with a smile. "Grandfather said it would happen, but I didn't know whether to believe him or not."

"I don't want to fight any battles that aren't mine," John said. "When you do, you never win, and it's just too much work."

"You're right," Josh said. "Let's go ask the Kingson what we should do. He always knows what's best." The children on old red bicycles pedaled slowly away from town down Cemetery Road. But they all watched the black truck in their rear view mirrors on their bicycles.

The man in the black derby looked into the rear view mirror as the truck sped for town. He smiled as he tapped some cigar ashes into a cup of brown liquid.

"The little brats are turning around and leaving," the man said. "I thought that Kramar boy might have recognized me. They don't want to tangle with me again."

"Hmmmpftt! I bet they're quaking in their shoes. Ha!" the old woman said sarcastically.

"You don't think they're scared of facing me again?" the man spat out. "I suppose you think you did a better job."

"You forget who served whom last summer," the old woman said. "And you better keep your mind on your business and get ahead of that girl or else you'll be demoted to a snail instead of a crow."

"Why the Bureau stuck me with you again I'll never know," the man muttered. He stepped on the gas as the truck passed the running girl.

Tiffany turned down North Main Street. She was planning on heading straight for home. That's when she saw the old woman pushing a brand-new Goliath UltraFlight bicycle. The woman had a kind face and reminded her of Granny Smith.

"Young girl," the old woman said. "I have something here that I think you'd be interested in."

Tiffany stopped. The bicycle looked just like the one she'd been riding.

"You misplaced this earlier," the old woman said. "You need to take it on back to the community center before you're missed."

"But where did you get it?" Tiffany asked. "I thought. . . ."

"It was by the side of the road in the fog."

Tiffany felt very confused. She took the bike. The woman smiled and then walked over to a parked black truck. She got inside and the truck drove away.

"This is really odd," Tiffany said. Not being sure what to do, she hopped on the bike and pedaled it back to the community center. She began to fume inside when she saw Sloan up on the stage, smiling and acting like a big shot. Tiffany pedaled up to the stage. All her friends cheered. They helped her get the bike on the stage. Standing next to Sloan, she smiled at the crowd, but then turned to Sloan.

"What happened to you?" she demanded of Sloan. "Why didn't you come back to me when I called you?"

"What do you mean?" Sloan replied.

"I mean in that place with the castle!"

"What castle?"

"Sloan, I saw you there," Tiffany said. "I gave you the Wildbird Drops so you could get back, but then you left me."

"The show must go on, as they say," Sloan said.

"But I could have been killed back there," Tiffany said.

"Back safe and sound," Professor Pickie said with a big handsome smile. "I think you two are SuperStar candidates for sure. People from the local newspaper are here to take your picture and learn about your first exciting journey."

"Oh," Tiffany said weakly.

"You will tell them how good it was, won't you?" the professor said, looking deeply into her eyes. He waited, watching her. Tiffany swallowed. She could tell that the professor only wanted a good story.

"It was great!" Tiffany said, forcing herself to smile.

"I knew it would be," the professor said. "Right this way."

Tiffany and Sloan were both smiling for the photographer as they stood by the UltraFlight bicycles. As the people in the crowd cheered, Tiffany began to feel like a star again. For a moment she felt the pain of an unusual weight around her neck. She immediately thought of the chain. She reached up, but her fingers touched only skin. Yet even the cheering crowd wouldn't make the uneasy feeling go away.

MARKED
FOR LIFE

6

Every kid in town was back at the community center the next day. Professor Pickie had announced that there would be a special movie presentation and that there would be free test rides on the Goliath UltraFlights for everyone who wanted a ride. Those who had missed the previous day's exhibition had heard all about it before the day was over. They were all waiting in a group for the center to open. The big tractor-trailer truck was still in the parking lot, as was the stage.

Sloan and Tiffany were in the group closest to the front door of the community center. Sloan was bragging to his friends about the wonders and powers of the UltraFlight as they waited. Tiffany listened with growing irritation.

"I felt like a real prince," Sloan said to his friend Jason. "You can't really imagine the sensation until you get up in the air on an UltraFlight yourself."

"Wow," Jason said. The other kids in Sloan's Commando Patrol nodded. Each one was envious.

"It seemed a little shaky on the takeoff," George Booth said.

"Naw," Sloan said. "Smooth as silk."

"I thought it was kind of bumpy," Tiffany said. "My bike was shaking all over the place. For a while, I thought my teeth would be rattled right out of my mouth."

"Really?" George said.

"I don't know if those bikes are very stable," Tiffany said.

"You're just scared because you're a weenie," Sloan said and laughed.

"I am not," Tiffany said. She didn't try to argue with her brother. She rarely won an argument with him. He always had a smart comeback. And that morning he was more determined than ever to sound as if he knew what he was talking about since he had been the first one to ride one of the strange new bicycles. Sloan loved to be the expert, and this was a great opportunity.

Tiffany was about to talk about the strange place she had flown to on the UltraFlight when a man opened the front doors of the community center. Everyone rushed in. Tiffany ran with the others to get a seat near the front in the auditorium. The place filled up fast with children and their parents. The balcony soon filled, too. A big white movie screen was hanging down from the ceiling. When everyone was seated, Professor Pickie walked out onto the stage. Everyone clapped. He smiled his handsome smile, his tanned face wrinkled with pleasure.

"Not many towns in this country are as lucky as Centerville," Professor Pickie said. "I have some important news for you all. Many of you have heard rumors, I'm sure, about the new changes in the Point System. Centerville has been chosen to be among the first set of towns and communities where Goliath and ORDER have teamed up to streamline the Point System with Number Marking."

 "I just wish the ranking would work on the system the way it is now," Tiffany whispered to Mary Ann.

"Me too," her friend replied. Sloan looked down the aisle of chairs and frowned at his sister for talking. Tiffany stuck her tongue out at her brother.

"Some of these changes may seem complicated, but they really are simple," the professor continued. "To help you understand, Goliath has made a film about what will be taking place in the future. So let's look at the film."

The lights went out and a film began to play on the big screen. Pictures of number cards filled the screen, which faded into Big Boards. The title came on the screen: *MARKED FOR LIFE!* "Everyone around the world knows how much easier and more efficient life has become since we've shifted to the Point System," a voice said while pictures of people from countries all around the globe were shown using number cards and Big Boards.

"And now, the greatest advancement and newest technology of all has been developed by Goliath Industries, Giants of Progress," the voice continued. "Number cards made great advances in fighting crime and reducing waste and saving time in all business transactions. With cash gone, and crime down, we entered a new age of peace and safety all over the world. Now we can make a good thing better. What if you lose your number card, or leave it at home when you go to the store? What if someone steals your card and tries to use it without your knowledge? Even though a stolen card is virtually impossible to use, it's still inconvenient."

There was a picture of a boy and girl in front of a Big Board. When they reached for their number cards, they both had forgotten or misplaced them. They looked upset. Some of the kids in the audience giggled.

"Goliath never rests until we achieve perfection in all our products and systems, and starting this summer, ORDER will introduce a major innovation by introducing the Number Mark."

The familiar circled white X filled the screen. Then it shrank down smaller and smaller until it you could see that the mark was in the center of a man's hand, in his palm, no bigger than the size of a pea.

"The Number Mark will perfect an already wonderful Point System. Everybody in the world will be Number Marked. Thanks to Goliath's new technology, it's a simple process. You will all receive a special number card biochip in your right hand or for those who prefer, on your forehead. This new six hundred series biochip, known as the Dragon 66, will clear up any and all bugs in the Point System Plus. When you are Number Marked, you never have to worry about losing or forgetting your number card. Nor do you have to worry about its being stolen because you are marked for life! No one can get your personal identification number mixed up."

"What about Big Boards?" a lady on the screen asked a man in a white laboratory coat.

"Big Boards will operate the same, except they will use hand or head scans instead of the old number card slots. There's even a new Hand Board digital radio-wave hookup, almost ready for sale. It will be like a personal Big Board, no bigger than a book." The screen showed a man using something that looked like a computer notebook. "With a Hand Board, you can get a Point System Breakdown, Rank Score, Buy/Sell Transaction printout and many more services any time you want. The future looks brighter every day when you get Number Marked. Soon, you too can be Marked for Life!"

The film ended in a rush of music and drums. Everyone clapped when it was over. Professor Pickie came back on stage.

"The little film you saw will help prepare you for a great future," the professor said. "In order to help publicize the new Number Marking process, Goliath and ORDER decided to do an entertaining action film. That's why I've come to Centerville. We want to make a great film here, called *The Mark of Perfection*."

The kids in the audience began talking among themselves. Tiffany and Mary Ann both began to feel more and more excited.

"We'll start filming on July Fourth," Professor Pickie said. "Since we start auditioning tomorrow, the fifteenth, all the roles should be cast in two weeks. This includes the lead parts as well as many others."

"Of course, we'll need lots of extras from the town," he said with a smile. The crowd of people murmured and nodded their heads. "And for realism, we'll be filming scenes of you all actually going through the new Number Marking process itself on July Fourth. That's important, so people can see how easy it is. It will be a historic moment in this community. After everyone is Marked, Goliath plans the biggest fireworks celebration this town has ever seen. This will be a new kind of Independence Day, as this and many other communities find new freedom through technological advances and get Number Marked for Life!"

"Will it hurt?" a little boy on the front row asked.

"Oh, it may sting a bit, but we'll provide a temporary painkiller for those who are worried," Professor Pickie said. "It won't sting for long, but the effects will last for life."

"What's the movie going to be about?" a little girl asked.

"I know you're all anxious to hear the story," Professor Pickie said. "So here it goes. Picture this. A young boy and girl live in a small town much like Centerville. These children are popular, but not famous or rich. You might even call them poor, but they're eager to rise to the top. They want the best for their town, for their government, and for ORDER around the world. Even though they're from a small town, they're concerned for the whole world, for peace and safety, for the environment, for making the world a better place. In short, they're for ORDER and progress. But not everyone is going along with the plan. Another group of people lives in this town, and they are trying to cause trouble."

"Bad guys," the children said.

"That's right. Bad guys," Professor Pickie repeated. "These people don't want progress. They even want to prevent people from getting Number Marked and using number cards."

"Sounds like those Rank Blank kind of people," Sloan said loudly. The other kids around him laughed.

"I knew Goliath had come to the right town," the man said. "You kids are perceptive and bright. They told me this town was above average."

All the children looked at each other and smiled. Each one knew in his or her heart that they were among the above average group.

"Anyway, this town is making progress, until this group of Rank Blank troublemakers tries to take over," Professor Pickie said. "First, they try to take over the schools and the stores, and then they try to take over the government and the police force.

"Now, this little boy and girl think that they can't do anything because they are just kids and not old like grownups," Professor Pickie continued. "But really they are the chosen ones to help save the town. In fact, they don't know it, but a long, long time ago they descended directly from a magnificent kingdom, back when there were castles and knights and warriors and brave princesses. In fact, they might even have been the true prince and princess themselves in another life."

"Golly," Mary Ann whispered. "I always thought I used to be a real princess in another life. And if I wasn't, I should have been."

"Really?" Tiffany asked with surprise. "I don't believe people live their lives over and over. It doesn't make sense. I think you'd really remember if that were true."

"These children, the stars of our movie, think they are so ordinary that they can't help do anything about the bad people causing trouble," Professor Pickie said. "But then they discover the Goliath UltraFlight bicycles. Now, they don't know how powerful these bicycles really are. But in one of the most exciting parts of the movie, the superhero boy and the superhero girl are transported back in time to this castle fairy-land as they ride the Goliath UltraFlight bicycles. Once back in time in their family's kingdom, they discover their true heritage as superheroes, a true prince and princess. They fight dragons and help prevent some wicked knights from taking over the castle. The townspeople love them and reward them for being the greatest heroes living in the land."

"Wow!" Mary Ann said. "Sounds dreamy after all." Tiffany didn't say anything, but she was a bit uncomfortable with how familiar it sounded.

"Once they discover their true heritage, the Goliath UltraFlights bring them back to the present time," Professor Pickie said. "This time they don't act like cowards, but like a prince and princess. With their Goliath UltraFlight bicycles leading the way, they ride into power. They confront the Rank Blank Spirit Flyer people from the air and destroy the rebellion. The townspeople are free once again to be part of ORDER and to progress. The government, of course, recognizes their bravery and heroism. They are rewarded handsomely with lots of units in the Point System, not to mention an extremely high ranking for life. The whole world wants to know the story of these young heroes, so they go to Hollywood to make a movie, and that's where they live, happily ever after, true SuperStars and superheroes. And that's the end."

The children all clapped and whistled. Tiffany pushed aside her doubts because something deep inside told her that she was born to play the part of the girl who becomes a princess.

"Maybe I was a princess in another life," Tiffany said.

"Maybe you'll be a princess again," Mary Ann said. She knew Tiffany was most likely to be the one to succeed. "Maybe I can be the princess's sister? You think they'd let me? I bet if you told them I was your best friend they'd let me. Will you ask them?"

"I haven't got the part yet," Tiffany said, blushing with pleasure. All the girls in her group looked down the row and smiled at her. Tiffany was sure that she could win the starring role.

"Maybe I should be your other sister," Jennifer said. "After all, I'm one of your best friends too."

"I asked first, Jennifer," Mary Ann said. "Didn't you hear me?"

"Well, I have just as much right to be the princess's sister as you do,"

Jennifer pouted. "I don't see why you should get the part. After all, I was higher on the Point System than you for several months."

"But when the system stopped working, I was ranked five points above you," Mary Ann said. "So you can forget about getting a better role than me."

"Maybe the princess can have a whole court of servants who are really her friends," Sharon said. "Then we could all sort of be in it. What do you think, Tiffany?"

"Well, I'm not sure if the director will let me decide those things or not," Tiffany said. "But if I'm the star, I should have some say, don't you think?"

"I think so," Mary Ann said. "The real stars always get to make all kinds of demands and things. Like riding around in limousines. Will you take us for a limousine ride when the film opens in Hollywood? I want to sit in the front seat with you."

"Why should you get to sit in the front seat of the limousine?" Jennifer asked. "After all, I'm just as much a friend as you, and I was ranked higher in the Point System for a longer time."

"Now I know you all are excited about signing up for the auditions for this great new movie, *The Mark of Perfection,*" Professor Pickie said. Everyone clapped and cheered. "But to do that, you need to go back out to the stage area by the truck. Our helpers with give you the necessary forms that you and your parents need to fill out. So please meet me outside. Besides the forms, we have an extra treat for you. We know you all want to take a ride on Goliath's new UltraFlight bicycle. And today, your dream may just come true."

With those words, everyone got up in a hurry. There was a stampede for the doors. Everyone wanted to take a ride on the mysterious bikes.

THE CHASE
IS ON
. . . .
7

Tiffany rushed outside with her friends. Everyone was excited when they saw not one or two, but more than thirty of the black and gold Goliath UltraFlights on the stage. And more were being rolled out of the back of the long tractor-trailer truck.

Several men in gray Commando uniforms were handing out paper folders with forms inside. Tiffany took hers. She decided to look at it later. Like most of the kids, she pressed close to the stage to look at the UltraFlight bikes.

"Look who's coming!" Mary Ann said in surprise. Tiffany turned. Josh Smedlowe, John Kramar, Susan Kramar, Daniel Bayley and Amy Burke all rode up on their old red Spirit Flyer bicycles. Tiffany was surprised they came in so close. Most of the time the kids with Spirit Flyer bicycles stayed in the distance. But unlike many of the kids with Spirit Flyer bikes, Josh Smedlowe was not one to hang back from the crowds. Since he lived right across the street from the Favors in the Smedlowes' home, Tiffany usually saw him every day or two, even though he had started going to the private school out at the Kramar farm during the last quarter of the school year.

Josh didn't seem to be afraid of anything or anyone. In the past, he and Sloan had even had run-ins with each other. She knew her brother hated Josh with a passion since Josh had successfully defended himself in a fight at school. Ever since then, Sloan had vowed to get even with Josh one day, but so far that day had never come.

"What are you doing here?" Sloan called out to Josh.

"We just came to look at what was going on," Josh said calmly.

"Well, you can just take off, right now," Sloan said.

"This is a free country," Josh said. "At least it's supposed to be free. If we want to watch, we can."

"I told you to get out of here," Sloan repeated. He looked around to make sure all the other boys in his Commando Patrol were nearby. They all crowded in closer to Sloan and glared at Josh.

Professor Pickie came outside and stepped onto the stage. He looked with interest at the group of five children with Spirit Flyer bicycles. He called over a few men in ORDER Security Squad uniforms. He whispered something to them. The men nodded and then walked into the back of the truck.

"As I mentioned inside, I know many of you are anxious to take a test ride on a Goliath UltraFlight," Professor Pickie announced. The crowd of children clapped. Sloan and his friends turned away from Josh to listen.

"Just what makes those bicycles go?" Josh asked the white-haired man. The children on Spirit Flyer bicycles watched, listening.

"Are you some kind of reporter?" Professor Pickie asked, looking down.

"Yes," Josh said simply. "I'm writing about this new movie. Can anyone come to the auditions?"

"Of course," Professor Pickie said.

"We're thinking we might like to be in it," Josh said. "Maybe we could audition like the other kids."

"You children audition?"

"Sure, why not?"

"Do you have number cards?" Professor Pickie asked. All the kids on red bikes frowned. They had heard the question many times before.

"No," Josh said simply.

"Then you must realize you can't audition without a card," Professor Pickie said. "No card, no audition."

"But why?" Josh insisted. "Why do we have to have a card to do everything? Why can't ORDER just accept us as we are?"

"Because you're different from the majority," Professor Pickie said. "You minorities just don't like progress or want peace and safety. Everyone must conform or life becomes too messy."

"Yeah," Sloan echoed. "Why don't you troublemakers just leave us all alone?"

"Maybe we just want our freedom," Josh said. "Why does everyone have to be the same? Why isn't there room enough for all of us? It's a big world, isn't it?"

"Not as big as it used to be," the professor said. "Besides, it's been proven you Rank Blank people are not loyal to ORDER. We can't have disorder and have a safe world."

"So you want to get rid of anything that doesn't conform to your ideas or policies," Josh said.

"This conversation is getting old," Professor Pickie said. "These children came out here to ride on the UltraFlights."

"Why don't you tell us what makes the bikes run?" Josh asked. "You avoided that question."

Professor Pickie was quiet. He stared at Josh for a moment. Four men walked out of the back of the truck with large boxes.

"I need volunteers on the stage to try out the UltraFlights," Professor Pickie said. Everyone rushed for the stage. Over forty kids got on the UltraFlight bicycles. Each child was given a red tube of Wildbird Energy Drops. Tiffany and Mary Ann both got on the sleek new bikes. Tiffany was nervous, but she didn't want anyone to think she was afraid.

"Most of you saw how the bicycles worked yesterday," Professor Pickie said. "Sloan Favor can demonstrate."

Sloan smiled as he rolled his bicycle to the front of the stage. He put the Wildbird Drops on the black TRAG-Ultra 7 box attached to the handlebars. As before, the tube was sucked deep inside the mysterious box. All over the stage, the children watching did the same as Sloan. Tiffany gulped and put her tube of Wildbird Drops on the box. It disappeared in an instant. Everyone put his or her right hand on the box and pulled it away quickly when each was stuck by the tiny needle inside the black box.

Josh and the other kids with Spirit Flyer bikes watched with interest. Sloan whispered to the men in the Security Squad uniforms. Then he looked back at Josh.

"What's in those glass tubes?" Josh called up to Professor Pickie.

"That's a trade secret," the professor said, trying to ignore the boy.

"Is that what makes them run?" Josh asked again. The professor acted as if he didn't hear him. Josh turned to his friends.

"Let's look a little deeper. Turn on your lights!"

All together the children on the old red bicycles flipped on the lights on the handlebars of their bicycles. For an instant, there was a flash of light. Tiffany saw a long dark chain on Mary Ann. In fact, everyone on the stage seemed to be wearing a chain. But the strangest sight of all was the professor.

As soon as the lights came on, he yelled out, as if he was hurt. He covered his face. But even with his hands up as a shield, Tiffany could still see behind them. She rubbed her eyes. For an instant, the professor's head looked exactly like that of a large hooded snake.

"Get those brats!" the professor shouted. Suddenly, there seemed to be chaos on the stage. Out of nowhere, someone threw a Slime Ball at Josh. The first one missed, but a second hit him in the chest. Big green gobs of goop slid down his chest. Sloan yelled out a war cry. Everyone was grabbing Slime Balls and Faster Blasters from the Security Squad people. Many of them were getting back packs and front packs to carry their weapons.

"Let's see what makes these Rank Blanks run!" Sloan shouted out. He threw a Slime Ball as hard as he could throw. It exploded against Susan Kramar's shoulder.

Josh and the other kids on the Spirit Flyer bikes turned and began to pedal away when they saw how outnumbered they were.

"Load up!" Sloan yelled. "It's time we took care of these trouble-makers once and for all!"

Like everyone else, Tiffany grabbed a pack full of Slime Balls and a Faster Blaster. The children on Spirit Flyers were just leaving the parking lot when Sloan and the others began pedaling. The UltraFlights leaped off the stage and shot into the air. Tiffany and Mary Ann and everyone else began to follow.

"Let's hunt them down and destroy them!" Sloan yelled out, looking over his shoulder. He held up a Slime Ball in his hand, but the children on the Spirit Flyer bikes were out of range. He stood up on his pedals to go faster. The air was filled with the UltraFlights. Shooting across the parking lot, ten feet up in the air, they looked like a swarm of giant, black and gold wasps.

Tiffany pedaled as fast as she could. Even though everyone was pedaling hard, the children on the old red bicycles stayed easily out of range. All the other kids were yelling and swearing as they chased the Rank

Blanks. But they couldn't close the distance. They chased the Spirit Flyer children all the way to the other side of Centerville, down Cemetery Road and past the factory. But the red bikes still outran the UltraFlights even though the Spirit Flyers were still rolling along on the ground.

Up ahead, the children on the Spirit Flyer bikes stopped. Tiffany was surprised. She wondered if they were going to turn and fight. But what would they fight with, she wondered. They didn't have any Slime Balls or any other weapons.

"They're still coming," John Kramar said, looking over his shoulder.

"They can't catch us on those crates," Josh said.

"But what should we do?" Susan asked. "I hate to just make them madder."

"Let's get up in the air to see what they'll do," Josh said, looking back. "Maybe they'll get tired and go home."

The kids on the Spirit Flyers began to pedal. One by one, the old red bicycles rose into the air.

"Did you see that?" Mary Ann asked. "Their bikes fly too."

"I've seen them do it before," Tiffany said.

"Golly, look how fast they go," Sharon called out. Everyone in the group of swarming UltraFlights was talking to each other and pointing as they saw the old red bicycles begin to fly.

"After them!" Sloan yelled back at his companions. His voice was hoarse, and he was sweating from pedaling so hard. Tiffany watched in surprise. She had hardly ever seen Sloan sweat. But she had hardly ever seen him more determined. He was desperate to catch up with Josh.

Tiffany followed the group as they flew higher into the air. She held on tightly to the handlebars of the UltraFlight. For ten minutes they followed, yet they still weren't any closer. They went far out into the country, over forests and farms and trees. Then suddenly, those on the Spirit Flyer bikes circled around and stopped still in the air, facing their pursuers.

"They're giving up!" Sloan yelled. Sensing that victory would soon be

his, he pedaled faster. His UltraFlight shook and wobbled as it moved through the sky. When they were about fifty yards away, Tiffany heard blowing horns that seemed to be coming from the Spirit Flyers. It sounded eerie to the girl. She slowed down. She suddenly knew deep in her heart that the horns were a warning of some kind. She wasn't sure how she knew, but she knew.

"I think we better slow down," Tiffany yelled over to Mary Ann. "Something's not right."

"Are you kidding?" Mary Ann shouted. "We can blast them right out of the sky."

Sloan stood up on his pedals. He had a Slime Ball cocked in his right hand, ready to throw. Just when he and the others at the front of the group were almost in range, the lights came on, hitting them like a wave. Sloan dropped the Slime Ball.

"I feel so weak," Tiffany said.

"I feel so heavy," Mary Ann called out. Tiffany looked at her friend. Once more, she saw the dark chain connected to a ring around her friend's neck. All the UltraFlights slowed and stopped. Then they began to sink. The crystal gear levers began to blink red. The children all started shouting in fear and frustration as the bikes dropped slowly from the sky. Some turned and headed toward town. A wind seemed to come up from nowhere. The group of kids on UltraFlights were blown across the sky like dandelion seeds.

Tiffany yelled as her bike descended. She found herself far away from any of her friends. She looked down. She was right on top of a farm. A white house with blue trim and several other buildings were near a road. Out in the field she saw tents and trailers and a small shack. As her bike fell further, she realized that this was the Kramar farm.

"Oh, no," she moaned. But there was nothing she could do. The bike kept slowly falling. She landed right behind a large barn near an old stone well. Before she could think what to do, Josh Smedlowe and the other Rank Blank kids were swooping down on her. She thought about reaching for a Slime Ball and her Faster Blaster, but she realized she was outnumbered. None of her friends on UltraFlights were near her.

"Leave me alone!" Tiffany said as the old red bikes touched down on the ground around her.

"We don't want to hurt you," Josh said. "If we had wanted to fight, we would have tried something back in town."

"We're your friends, Tiffany," Susan Kramar said softly. "I know you probably don't believe us. But the kings brought you here for a reason. All the others were blown back toward town."

"Why me?" Tiffany said. "What do you want? I just want to leave."

"You can leave any time," Josh said. But Tiffany was suspicious. She didn't understand these kids. They had been attacked just a few minutes ago, but they didn't seem to be angry. More than anything, they seemed puzzled and somewhat curious.

"This is the farm they call the Rank Blank Town, isn't it?" Tiffany asked.

Josh and the other kids smiled.

"That's what some people call it," John Kramar said. "To me it's just home. There are a lot of people staying here, though. Last time we counted there were over a hundred."

"But how do you do it?" Tiffany asked. She was feeling less afraid since she began to see that they didn't really intend to hurt her. "I mean, how can you survive without number cards? You can't buy anything without a number card."

"The Three Kings provide," Susan Kramar said. "We can grow things, but we can also trade and barter for things we need and can't buy. There are a lot of people who have number cards who are old friends. And real friends don't desert their friends, no matter what those ORDER people say. A lot of people in town think the Point System is unfair, even though they still use number cards."

Tiffany looked around. Both children and adults were out working in the fields. Some children were playing. As she watched them, something about the farm seemed very peaceful. "I better go back to town," Tiffany said softly. "Professor Pickie will be wanting this bicycle back."

"It's a mistake to hang around that guy," Josh Smedlowe said. Once again Tiffany was surprised. Josh didn't seem to be accusing her. He actually seemed to be concerned. "Goliath and ORDER are up to no good. We think the whole town is going to be tricked by them."

"I've got to go now," Tiffany said. She looked away from Josh's brown eyes.

"We can show you how to get rid of your chain, Tiffany," Susan Kramar said.

"I've got to go," Tiffany said more forcefully. For some reason she felt like she was going to cry, and she didn't want them to see. She began pedaling the UltraFlight for the driveway.

"Wait!" Josh called. He rode over to her. He held out his hand and opened it. Tiffany almost gasped when she saw her necklace and locket that Granny Smith had given her. "I keep forgetting to give this back to you. The chain was broken, but I fixed it."

"Thank you," Tiffany said. She stared at the necklace in surprise. "But how . . . ," she started to say. She had almost convinced herself that her time inside the crumbling castle had been some kind of dream. As she took the necklace, she shivered, feeling even more confused. "I really need to leave."

As she rode down the gravel driveway, she was surprised that Josh or the others didn't follow her or call out to her. Deep inside, she realized that she was disappointed at their silence. She wanted them to pursue her for some reason.

"I must be going crazy," Tiffany said to herself as she turned onto Glory Road. She looked back. They were all sitting on their bikes in front of the white and blue house, watching her. Tiffany pedaled faster. As soon as she was out of sight, she began to cry. She wasn't sure why. She pedaled down the old country road with blurry eyes. "Nothing makes sense," she thought again. "Nothing makes sense at all."

AUDITIONS
· · · · · · · ·

8

Tiffany woke up early on Monday morning, but she was still the last one up. She wore her pajamas downstairs.

"Make sure you eat a good breakfast," Mrs. Favor said. "But don't overdo it. You want to have plenty of energy for your audition. But you don't want to feel too heavy."

"I won't feel heavy," Tiffany said. She felt tired. She hadn't slept well the night before. That bright star in the sky kept shining in her window, making it hard for her to fall asleep. And she kept thinking about her two journeys on the UltraFlight bicycles. She was still puzzled about Josh and the other Rank Blank kids. She hadn't told any of her friends about landing at the farm. All the other children she had talked to had landed on country roads much closer to town. Tiffany thought that was odd. None of them had been hurt either.

Though neither Sloan nor any of his friends would admit it, Tiffany was sure that a power or something had driven the UltraFlights away. The whole incident had been no contest. The UltraFlights were slower and didn't have a chance of catching up with the old red bicycles. That was just one of the many things that had Tiffany baffled. She ate her breakfast silently.

Afterward, she dressed in a nice pair of tan pants and a white blouse. With a great deal of effort, her mother got her hair to stay down. Tiffany wore makeup and a light shade of lipstick.

"Don't put on too much," her mother said. "It said in the forms that they would apply their own makeup. Sloan is already down there. Your father took him."

"Ok," Tiffany said without enthusiasm. She realized that she wasn't looking forward to the audition. Part of her felt nervous. But part of her was worried about Josh's warnings. She couldn't stop thinking about them. And she couldn't stop thinking about those strange chains that she kept seeing on herself and others.

"It's all in my imagination," Tiffany said. She reached up and touched her neck. Granny Smith's golden necklace and locket was still there. Tiffany immediately thought of Josh and his strong brown eyes. She also thought about Granny Smith, whom she hadn't seen in a while. She'd have to make a visit soon.

"Let's go," her mother called out. Tiffany let go of the necklace and ran downstairs. She rode in the back seat without speaking. In a few minutes they drove through the Goliath factory gate.

"The auditions are here?" Tiffany asked.

"Sure," Mrs. Favor said. "They're using that new warehouse as a place for the sets."

Tiffany followed her mother into the warehouse. They walked down a hall and then into a large open room. She gasped when she saw the castle and moat and town in the distance. Everything looked just as it did when she rode the UltraFlight the first time. Bright lights shone on the scene, making everything seem even brighter than daytime. Several of Tiffany's friends were sitting in chairs in the shadows, watching the auditions. Tiffany and her mother went over and sat down with the others.

"Cut!" a voice shouted. Sloan stepped out of the castle door wearing a king's costume with a large, flowing hat.

"Try the crown," Professor Pickie said loudly. A man ran out from behind the wall, took away the hat and put a crown on Sloan's head.

"I like this," Sloan said. He walked grandly down the bridge that hung over the moat.

"Keep walking, keep walking . . . ," Professor Pickie called to Sloan. A big camera was aimed at the boy. "Keep that royal look, that kingly stance. You've definitely got star quality, my boy, star quality indeed."

"Of course," Sloan said, planting his feet firmly and looking off toward the town.

"He looks like he owns the town," Mary Ann said with admiration. "I bet Sloan gets the starring boy's part for sure."

"Probably," Tiffany said.

"Get into your costumes, girls," Professor Pickie said. He pointed them to a room off to the left. "Just put them over your clothes. That will do for the test."

Tiffany's mother walked right behind her as they went into the room. Tiffany looked at all the colorful costumes with admiration. She picked up a blue gown.

"Not that one, dear," Mrs. Favor said. She held up a shiny white gown with pearly beads. "Try this one. I think it looks more regal, and it will show off your complexion better."

Tiffany pulled on the beautiful gown. She stared in the full-length mirror, surprised at how beautiful she could look—and so suddenly, just by putting on a dress.

"You certainly look like a princess," Mrs. Favor said, but she wasn't happy and Tiffany could tell.

"What's wrong?" Tiffany demanded.

"It's just that your hair sticks up a little too much, even after all that work we did before we came," her mother replied. She searched on the shelves and found a smaller crown that seemed to be covered with diamonds. She slipped it over Tiffany's head.

"There, that's better," Mrs. Favor said. "You're definitely star quality now. Now remember, if they ask you to talk, speak up loudly and clearly. Only don't shout. You'll sound strained."

"Oh, Mother," Tiffany said.

"Do you want the part or not?" Mrs. Favor asked, not trying to hide the exasperation in her voice. "Did you see how Sloan walked and spoke?"

"He looks like he's strutting," Tiffany said.

"Royalty do strut because they have something to strut about," her mom said. "You're a princess, so you have to walk like a princess."

Tiffany looked at the beautiful gown. The jewels on the crown glistened and sparkled. Still, something seemed to be missing.

"I don't feel like a princess," Tiffany said flatly. "I don't know what's wrong with me."

"I don't either," Mrs. Favor replied. "What kind of attitude is that? This could be one of the most important events of your life. Now get out there and show them who's the best girl in town. Win that part."

Tiffany shuffled down toward the stage. A man motioned for her to come in a side door into the castle. She walked toward the light of the doorway. Then the lights hit her face. They were so bright that they were blinding. But in the glow, she began to feel like a star.

"Maybe this is how movie stars feel, with everyone looking at them, telling them where to stand and where to walk," Tiffany thought. It felt fun to have so much attention focused on her.

"Test one, Tiffany Favor," a voice yelled out, and then she heard a clack.

"When I say 'Action,' walk *slowly* down to the drawbridge and pick up the basket of flowers," Professor Pickie said. "Throw the flowers one by one into the water of the moat. Ready. Action!"

Tiffany walked out of the castle's door and down to the moat. She looked nobly toward the town and then walked down to the draw-bridge.

"Cut!" the voice yelled. Professor Pickie walked in front of the lights. "This isn't a race, Tiffany. I want you to walk slowly. Remember, you're an ordinary girl who has discovered she really is a princess. Take time to enjoy that discovery. Now go back and start over."

Tiffany hurried up the steps back into the castle. Her mother was waiting on the other side of the door.

"Make sure you do what he says, Tiffany," Mrs. Favor said. "He said Sloan walked right through his whole audition without a hitch. I want him to know you can listen to directions and get this part."

"I'm trying, Mother," Tiffany said. "I wasn't sure how slowly he meant."

"Pretend you're a princess and you'll be a princess."

Tiffany pulled at her dress and arranged it. Mrs. Favor patted her hair and pushed the crown down tighter.

"Action!"

Tiffany walked out of the door into the blinding lights. She walked down the steps, telling herself to slow down, slow down. This time she didn't feel so noble and wasn't sure she liked all the attention focused on her. But she reached the drawbridge without the professor telling her to stop, and she felt better. She took the basket of flowers. She scooped up some in her arms, then smelled one, lingering. Then she tossed it away, over the edge of the drawbridge. One by one, she threw the flowers into the water.

"Great, great," Professor Pickie said off in the darkness. "Now lean over the edge of the drawbridge and look down into the water."

Tiffany put the basket on the edge and leaned over, looking down into the water. The flowers were floating away in the current. She stared wistfully into the water at her reflection. Then she saw it. In her reflection, a dark chain was hanging around her neck, attached to a metal collar. Tiffany leaned over to get a better look. The chain began to pull the face of her reflection under the water. For a moment Tiffany wasn't sure if she was looking at her reflection or a real girl being pulled under. The face in the water seemed to be in pain.

"Eaaaacck!" Tiffany screamed and jerked back from the edge of the bridge. She jumped so fast that her crown slipped off and began to fall. Tiffany scrambled to catch it, but it bounced out of her fingers and, before she could stop it, over the edge of the bridge. She heard a tiny splash.

"Cut!" Professor Pickie yelled. He stepped from behind the lights. "What's going on, Tiffany? You were doing great and you lost it."

"I don't know what happened," Tiffany said. "I saw that chain again. It was on the girl in the water."

"Chain? Girl in the water?" Professor Pickie asked. He looked at Tiffany as if she had two heads.

Mrs. Favor walked out of the castle and hurriedly down the steps. Tiffany could see right away that she was unhappy.

"Tiffany's been a little nervous lately," Mrs. Favor said sweetly. "This is her first time in front of cameras. She can do better on the next take. Can't you, honey?"

"Sure, I suppose so," Tiffany said. "But it looked so real . . . I mean the girl with the chain. I heard her say something. I'm sure of it."

"We have what we need on tape," Professor Pickie said. "Most of it looked really good. Especially where you sniffed the flowers before you threw them in the water. Mary Ann Mayberry is next. Quiet on the set as Mary Ann gets ready."

Tiffany walked slowly back to the costume room. She hung up the costume, and as she saw the crowns, she remembered all over again how foolish she felt. Her mother was unusually quiet. Tiffany was sure she was mad.

"What was going on in your mind, young lady?" Mrs. Favor asked. She was steaming inside, Tiffany could tell. "How could you scream, and then knock your crown in the water?"

"It just happened!" Tiffany said.

"Well, it better not happen again," Mrs. Favor said. "Do you want to be a star or not?"

"Of course I want to be a star," Tiffany said. "It's just . . . It's just . . . I don't know. I feel funny with the costume and the lights and everything."

"Well, we'll practice. I'll get your father to get us some of these costumes, and you can practice walking. Practice makes perfect. After all, this is a Goliath Company. I'm sure he can persuade Professor Pickie to let us practice on the stage in the off hours. You and Sloan both, if you need to catch up."

"Remedial walking? I have to practice walking?"

"Don't be sarcastic. You know what I mean, Tiffany. Walking in a costume, with a crown, like a little princess."

"Yes, Mother," Tiffany said. "Can I go now?"

"I suppose so," her mother said. "I need to talk to Professor Pickie about Sloan's part."

Her mother walked over to Professor Pickie. Everyone was watching Mary Ann's audition. Tiffany ran out of the warehouse.

"I guess I'll practice walking on the way home," she said to herself. "Maybe I'll be a star and maybe I won't."

The moment she said the word *star,* she looked up in the sky. High overhead that star hung motionless in the sky. Tiffany was sure it was growing bigger and getting closer. She frowned and began walking home.

GRANNY
SMITH

. . . .

9

Tiffany walked all the way home thinking about her audition. All she could see were the mistakes. She knew her mother was disappointed. As usual, Sloan had done the best job and come out ahead of her.

"I blew it. I just know it," Tiffany said. Then she thought of the chain she had seen in the water. Thinking about the chain made her feel scared. She thought of how she had dropped the crown. She was sure her whole family would be disappointed in her for not doing a perfect audition. The only one who wouldn't criticize her would be Granny Smith. When she got home, she knew what she wanted to do.

Tiffany got her Goliath Super Wings bike out of the garage. She rolled down the driveway and out onto Buckingham Street. She rode up Main Street to 12th and then went west toward Highway 63, which ran north and south. As the last houses of town began to disappear, she saw the highway and the Glory Road Retirement Home. Before she went inside, she looked up in the sky. The star hung eerily in the blackness. You could even see it faintly in the day now. It *was* getting bigger and brighter, she thought. Tiffany was sorry she had looked.

The home had been a motel several years before, until it had been turned into a retirement home. Granny Smith had her own little room and kitchen. There were rooms for individuals, plus some suites where two people shared several large rooms together—a bedroom, a kitchen and a living room.

Tiffany knocked on her door, but no one answered.

"Come on," Tiffany said. She knocked harder, wondering if Granny Smith could hear her. Still no answer.

Tiffany walked down to the office. She went through the doors of the lobby into the meeting hall. A big fireplace was at one end of a room. A woman with a nurse's cap was stationed at the reception desk. Tiffany looked around. Several older people were sitting in chairs talking.

"May I help you?" the receptionist asked.

"I'm looking for—"

"Tiffany!" a voice called. Granny Smith was at the far end of the room by a long table. She was waving at Tiffany.

"I came to see my Granny Smith," Tiffany said. The woman behind the desk smiled and nodded.

Tiffany walked quickly across the room. Granny Smith wasn't sitting at a table, as it turned out, but in front of a large, square piece of brightly decorated cloth.

"We're doing some quilting today," Granny Smith said with a smile as Tiffany came over. She stood up and gave Tiffany a big hug. Tiffany hugged back as hard as she could. Granny Smith had the best, strongest hug the girl had ever known.

"My, my, you feel like someone that needed a hug," Granny Smith said with a twinkle in her old, gray eyes.

"I do, I do," Tiffany blurted out. Tears began to come to her eyes. "I feel really confused and scared."

"Well, child, slow down and let me give you another hug," the old woman said. She leaned forward and held Tiffany again. The girl closed her eyes. Granny Smith always smelled nice and flowery, sort of like lavender and roses mixed together. She patted Tiffany on the back softly, as if she were a little girl. Part of Tiffany felt embarrassed to be treated that way, and part of her wished she could be a little girl again, a little, tiny girl about four or five years old. Then everyone would treat her nice again and life wouldn't be so confusing.

Tiffany held onto the old woman and looked down at the quilt through blurry eyes. The material was beautiful. In the center was a blazing star, which almost seemed to be moving across a blue, blue sky. On one edge of the quilt were three golden-colored crowns sewn into the fabric. Patchwork squares lined the borders of the quilt. The giant blanket appeared to be almost done. The other women around the quilting table looked on silently as Granny Smith held Tiffany, patting her on the back.

Tiffany heard the sound of a tractor chugging outside. The noise seemed pleasant in its own way. Life was definitely more peaceful in the Glory Road Retirement Home than in Centerville with all the action going on there about the big movie coming to town. An old man walked into the room and crossed over to where the women were quilting. He looked at Tiffany and smiled. He didn't say a word.

"What's worrying you, child?" Granny Smith asked softly.

"Everything!" Tiffany said. "That star everyone is talking about. And the movie coming to town, and we're supposed to audition. I did my audition this morning, and it was horrible. Nobody knows where they really stand because the Point System ranking isn't working. Nothing's working right. I was riding this new bicycle and all these strange things happened."

"You had a strange bike ride?" Granny Smith asked.

"Yes, but can we go someplace and talk about it?" Tiffany asked, beginning to feel embarrassed. She didn't want to talk in front of strangers.

"Let's go back to my room, then," Granny Smith said. She took the thimbles off her fingers and put them in her sewing bag. She stuck a needle into a pincushion.

"We need to be going back to the farm," the old man said to some of the ladies. A tall, gray-haired lady and a shorter lady stood up. Both smiled at Tiffany. Tiffany felt embarrassed all over again, especially when they all walked toward the front door at the same time.

"You ladies are making one of the finest quilts I've ever seen," the old man said.

"It'll still take a week more to get it done," the tall woman said. She had a brisk walk for someone her age, Tiffany thought. The old man opened the door for them all. Once outside, Tiffany was surprised to see the two older women and the old man all walk over to a red tractor. The tractor was idling with a pleasant chugging sound. The old man climbed on and, to Tiffany's surprise, both of the old women climbed up beside him. They sat on the big back wheel covers.

"Just a minute," Granny Smith said. She walked over to the tractor. She talked to her three friends for a few moments and then walked back. The big tractor chugged louder and turned slowly in the parking lot. The lights were on, and they seemed especially bright, almost hot as they shone on her while the tractor was turning. The lights were so bright, Tiffany closed her eyes and put her hand up to her face. She was sure she could feel the heat come off her face as the lights passed by. When she opened her eyes, the old people on the tractor were chugging out of the parking lot, heading west, away from town.

"Who were those people?" Tiffany asked as they walked to Granny Smith's room.

"Old friends of mine," the old woman said as she opened the door. "The tall woman is Thelma Kramar, and the man is John Kramar, her brother. The other woman is Lois Kramar, John's wife. They were neighbors of mine back home, before I moved down here. They stay at John's son's farm not too far from here. Thelma's one of my dearest friends. She has more gumption and energy than you and your brother put together, I imagine. I've never seen a woman get around so."

"Kramar," Tiffany said softly. "I wonder. . . ."

"Would you like some tea?" Granny Smith asked. She began making it before Tiffany even answered, because she knew the answer would be yes. Granny Smith made tea mixed with apple juice and cinnamon that was delicious.

"Of course," Tiffany said. "You know I always want two cups of your tea."

The old woman laughed and nodded as she turned on the gas stove. She poured water into the tea pot.

"Now why don't you tell me what's bothering you," the old woman said. As she put the kettle on the stove, Tiffany began her story. The old woman just listened as Tiffany told her about the movie and the auditions. Then she told her about her adventures on the UltraFlights and the castle. Granny Smith always listened intently. As she poured the tea, Tiffany told her about Josh Smedlowe and the other children with Spirit Flyer bikes.

"It was really scary. They just burst in on the place with the castle on those old bikes," Tiffany said. "I don't know how they got there or anything. And they talked about that chain I was telling you about. Those guys are really strange. No one likes them."

"Why not?" Granny Smith asked.

"Because they're Rank Blank," Tiffany said. "All those kids with those junky Spirit Flyer bikes are Rank Blank."

"Is that really so bad?"

"To be Rank Blank?" Tiffany asked. "Are you kidding? That's the worst, Granny. No one wants to be Rank Blank. They're considered enemies of ORDER and the government. They are positively evil. Do you know that they even have this illegal farm outside of town?"

"I've heard stories," the old woman said. "But what makes you think they're so evil? Have they ever done anything to hurt you? Or have they hurt anyone you know?"

"Well . . . I'm not sure," Tiffany said. "Josh Smedlowe punched Sloan one time. Of course, he was sort of defending his little retarded brother, Randy. And they scared me when they burst through into that place."

"But it sounds to me like they helped you escape," Granny Smith said. She nibbled on a small cookie. "You said Sloan left you there alone."

"He did, the rat," Tiffany said, feeling angry all over again. "Sloan always looks out just for himself."

"So the children with Spirit Flyer bikes never really harmed you, but you were still scared?" Granny Smith asked.

"I guess you could say that, except they kept talking about that chain, like they knew all about it," Tiffany said. "They act like they know everything."

"Maybe they do know something about that chain you saw," the old woman said. "Isn't that possible?"

"Well, sure, anything is possible, Granny, but they're Rank Blank," Tiffany emphasized. "You're not even supposed to talk to people like that or your points could go down. There's a kid named Roger Darrow who was in Sloan's patrol for a long time. He wasn't that smart, but he was rising up in the Point System. He was even getting close to the top ten, but then he started hanging around Josh Smedlowe and those Spirit Flyer kids and his rank went way, way down, almost overnight. Sloan had to make him leave the club. He's even one of them, now, we think. He hangs out with them all the time and just left all his old friends."

"I see," Granny Smith said, nodding her head. Tiffany took a long, delicious sip of tea. It tasted so soothing.

"Things aren't always what they seem," Granny Smith said slowly. "Maybe your friend Roger has found better friends. You said yourself, Sloan thinks only of himself."

"But he's Sloan," Tiffany said. "He's Number One. He can get away with it. People envy him, even if he isn't always friendly. He knows what's going on."

Granny Smith got up and walked over to a closet. She got something and returned. She handed Tiffany a small book with a dark brown cover. In the center of the cover were three golden crowns connected to each other. Tiffany opened the book to the title page.

"*The Book of the Kings?*" Tiffany asked in surprise. "I've heard of this book."

"Have you ever read any of it?" Granny Smith asked.

"No. I heard it was just a bunch of stories and fairy tales," Tiffany said. She frowned. "In fact, isn't this the book that all those Spirit Flyer people read?"

"Yes, it is," Granny Smith said. "It tells a lot about the Three Kings and their kingdom. It can also give you some answers about the chains you saw and even about the star that's come into our sky."

"Really?" Tiffany said eagerly.

"There's all kinds of wisdom in *The Book of the Kings,*" the old woman said. "But you have to be really reading and looking with your heart to see it. If you ask to see, the kings will show you what you need to know."

"Really?" Tiffany asked. It sounded like the best news she'd heard in several weeks. Suddenly there was a sharp pain in her neck. She reached her hand up to rub the sore place. The hope she had begun to feel quickly disappeared. She looked at the book and frowned. "I don't know. I mean, Mom and Dad don't want us to hang out with those Spirit Flyer people. I'm not sure they would like this book."

"Let me show you something," Granny Smith said, her eyes twinkling.

They walked slowly to the back of her small apartment. They went to the back door and then outside. They walked over to a small storage shed that looked like a little barn. Granny opened the two doors.

Tiffany blinked in surprise when she saw an old red bicycle parked in the shed. Granny Smith rolled the bike onto the sidewalk.

"It's a Spirit Flyer," Tiffany said softly. "But where did you get it?"

"All Spirit Flyers come from the kings," the old woman said.

"Did it cost a lot?" Tiffany asked. "I mean, it looks sort of old and junky. What do they cost new?"

"The Spirit Flyers are gifts that the kings give freely to whoever will receive," the old woman said. She patted the handlebars.

"So they don't cost anything?"

"They cost a great deal. In fact, they are priceless," Granny Smith said. "Freedom always comes at a great price to someone. In this case, the kings paid the price and then gave freely to those who would take their gifts in the spirit in which they were given."

"But . . . but . . . do my mother and father know about this?" Tiffany asked, suddenly feeling more than a little horrified. "You shouldn't have one of these, Granny. You could get into a lot of trouble. I mean, aren't you an enemy of ORDER if you have one of these?"

"I'm a servant of the kings and their kingdom," the old woman said. "I don't try to be anyone's enemy."

Tiffany looked at the old red bicycle in silence. She had never really gotten up close to a Spirit Flyer and looked at it before. She felt drawn to the mysterious old bike, but at the same time, she felt repelled by its ugliness.

"I don't think I could ever ride a bike like that," Tiffany said. "I mean, what would people think? What would Mom and Dad think? Sloan would hate it, and I would be an absolute zero on the Point System. I'd be Rank Blank. I'd be worse than zero. I'd have negative points."

"The Kingson became as nothing so we could become citizens of his kingdom," the old woman said softly. "Sometimes when you lose what seems precious in this world you gain something that is even more valuable."

"Does Mom know you have a Spirit Flyer?" Tiffany demanded, feeling more and more uncomfortable looking at the red bike.

"Your mother knows," Granny Smith said. "She doesn't approve, but she's always known. Your real grandmother, my sister, had one too."

"She did?" Tiffany asked in surprise. "But Mom never said anything. And you never told me before."

"The time just wasn't right," Granny Smith said. She rolled the bicycle back into the little storage shed and shut the doors. "But the time is getting short now. And I think you're getting to an age and a place in your heart where you won't settle for just playing the role of a princess in some cardboard kingdom in a movie of pretend. You can know the true kings and be their real child in a real kingdom that lasts forever and ever."

"Would I be a princess?" Tiffany asked.

"It wouldn't be quite like what I think you're thinking," the old woman said. "But you would be a child of the kings themselves. That's even better than anything you could imagine."

"But I want to be a star!" Tiffany said defiantly. "Professor Pickie said he thought I had star quality. I bet once I star in this movie, then I could be a star in Hollywood too. I could be known around the world as a star, and at a young age! It would be perfect."

"There's only one star," Granny Smith said. She pointed up into the sky. The star hung in the sky and seemed even bigger and closer to the girl. Deep inside, Tiffany felt disturbed. She wasn't sure if she was scared or what, but she wished the feeling would go away.

"I came here because you usually make me feel better," Tiffany said. "But I'm feeling more confused than ever. Why didn't you tell me you were one of them?"

"Tiffany, I love you and want you to have the best life you can," Granny Smith said. The old woman went inside. "I want you to have two things."

Granny Smith went over to a chest of drawers. She got a leather pouch about the size of a small purse. She came back over to Tiffany. She put the small copy of *The Book of the Kings* in the pouch.

"Here, I want you to have this copy," the old woman said. "But I have something else that is very special."

"What's that?" Tiffany asked without much enthusiasm.

"These goggles," Granny Smith said. From the pouch she pulled out a pair of old goggles that looked like the kind aviators wore a long time ago. Tiffany frowned when she saw them. Three tiny golden crowns were linked together in the middle. There was no way the old goggles would ever be in fashion. They were too old and goofy looking, she thought. On the side there were tiny words: *Spirit Flyer Vision.*

"But I don't need glasses or sunglasses for that matter," Tiffany said. "Besides, I could never be seen with those in public. I'd look like an absolute idiot. I'd lose a hundred points for sure."

"You don't have to wear these in public for them to work," Granny Smith said.

"But what are they for?"

"You could call them reading glasses or just something to see deeper with," the old woman said. "If you put these on and read *The Book of the Kings,* I think you'll begin to see the answers to some of your fears. And you'll see that the kings are more than names in a book, and much more real than fairy tales."

The old woman put the goggles back inside the worn leather pouch with the small book and pulled the drawstring tight.

Tiffany didn't want to hurt Granny Smith's feelings. She loved the old woman too much for that. So she took the pouch.

"I better go," Tiffany said. Granny Smith smiled. She hugged Tiffany one more time. Tiffany was so lost in her thoughts as she rode home that she didn't notice the small black truck following her.

The man in the black derby and the old woman with white hair followed Tiffany all the way to her home. They watched her go inside.

The man seemed especially interested in the leather pouch the girl was carrying.

"I can smell that junk from here," the man said, his face looking as if he would soon be sick.

"Me too," the old woman said. "Headquarters won't like this. We need to report to Cutright."

The black truck turned around and drove to the Goliath factory. The man in the derby and the old lady went inside the office building. A few moments later they were reporting everything they had observed to Mr. Cutright.

NEGA FLU
· · · · · · · ·
10

Tiffany stayed around her home most of the next couple of weeks. She heard stories about the children trying out for parts. All in all, she thought she was still the most likely candidate for the starring role of the princess. Her mother and father thought so too. Her mother talked about it every evening at the supper table. Tiffany got tired of hearing about it.

"You have to have follow through, Tiffany," her mother told her. "I push you kids a little because you won't push yourselves."

"I follow through," Sloan said.

"I know you do, dear," Mrs. Favor said.

"You mean I don't?" Tiffany accused. Once again she could feel the hot look of her mother's disapproval.

"You just don't have Sloan's drive," her mother replied lightly. "Maybe it's because he's a boy."

"That's not fair," Tiffany said.

"Well, I don't know what it is, but I do know this. You have to push a little if you want doors to open in this life. And sometimes I think you need a person there by your side to help you push."

"Thanks a lot," Tiffany said flatly.

"I'm just trying to help," her mother said sweetly.

And so it would go, more or less the same each night. Tiffany wanted to be a star, but she sure wished it was over. She'd lie in the bed in her room and cover herself with her stuffed animals, hoping they would somehow comfort her during the waiting process. But nothing seemed to work.

Tiffany walked through the days, practicing on her keyboard, going to gymnastics, and even going through math workbooks with a high school girl named Marcy Bright who was acting as a tutor. Normally Tiffany would have hated even the thought of having a tutor, especially during summer. But in these days before the final decision was announced about the audition, Tiffany was glad to keep her mind occupied.

She went to see Granny Smith almost every day. That was nice, except Tiffany felt guilty because she hadn't really looked at the book Granny had given her. Nor had she put on those odd, old goggles. But Granny Smith didn't pressure her to talk like her mother or her father. Tiffany just liked to be with her, sipping tea and doing crossword puzzles. On a few days she even got to help on the big quilt. And Granny Smith had also promised to teach her to knit. A few times, late at night, when no one was around, Tiffany would open her nightstand drawer and look at the leather pouch which held the book and goggles. But she always shut the drawer without opening the pouch.

Then two days before the auditions were over, on a Saturday, Tiffany opened the drawer and took out the leather pouch. She held it in her hands and felt peaceful because she thought of Granny Smith.

Tiffany opened the pouch and pulled out the book. She quickly opened it and began to read. At first it was confusing. As she had been told, the book was about the Three Kings. Tiffany was just about to close it when she saw the word *chains*. She kept reading and reading and reading, and before she knew it, the whole afternoon had gone, and she had read nearly to the end of the book.

Tiffany got up and walked back and forth in her room. She picked up the goggles lying on the bed by the pouch. She felt restless and more than a little bothered.

"Why did I even start reading that thing?" Tiffany muttered. But she kept thinking about what the book said about the chains. And it even mentioned a star. That was the hardest part to understand since the book seemed to talk in riddles and puzzles.

"I'm going for a ride," Tiffany said. Tiffany was about to throw the goggles on the bed but instead stuck them in her pocket.

She got her bike out of the garage and headed uptown. She rode up to the town square. Mary Ann and Sharon were sitting in the wooden gazebo, so Tiffany rode over. The two girls were looking at the old courthouse. Several men in gray ORDER Security Squad uniforms were carrying large dark panels through the front doors.

"What's going on?" Tiffany asked.

"We heard they are setting up the machine that will Number Mark people."

"Really?" Tiffany asked. She watched the men curiously.

"I can't wait," Mary Ann said. "They say once we get Number Marked that the Ranking part of the Point System will start working again. Then we'll all know where we rank, officially."

"My mother will be happy about that," Tiffany said.

"I wonder if it will hurt to get marked," Sharon said.

"I hope not," Mary Ann said. "You can have it done in your forehead or your hand, and I know I want my mark to be in my hand."

"Me too," Sharon said. "Where will you get marked, Tiffany?"

"I guess in my hand," Tiffany said slowly. She watched the men. She touched the old pair of goggles in her pocket. As they carried in more black panels and other equipment up the steps, she remembered reading something about marks in *The Book of the Kings*. Something about the whole scene made her feel uneasy.

"Jennifer said she is going to be Number Marked on the forehead, but I think she'll chicken out," Sharon said. "She was even too chicken to get a flu vaccination last year from the school nurse. Don't you think she's chicken, Tiffany?"

"I don't know," Tiffany muttered. "I better go now."

Tiffany hopped on her bike and rode away. The two girls in the gazebo watched her go.

"She seems to be in a strange mood," Mary Ann said.

"Yeah, well, she's probably just thinking how great she'll be in the movie," Sharon replied. "Sometimes I think Tiffany can be a real snob."

The two girls laughed and turned to watch the men in gray uniforms. Tiffany rode across the square by the music store. She thought she might go shopping, but then she decided she would go check on the auditions. She rode out to the factory. No one stopped her as she went inside the gate since the gatekeeper knew she was the vice president's daughter.

She rode over to the warehouse and parked her bike. She walked inside, but she didn't see anyone there. The place seemed to be strangely empty. One light was on and the castle set was dimly lit. She walked across the drawbridge and stepped onto the cobblestone streets of the set. A crown was sitting out on a metal folding chair. Tiffany put the crown on her head. As soon as she put it on, she felt like a star again. She began to get excited about the film.

She walked back inside the castle walls when she heard voices. Tiffany peeked out from behind the door. Professor Pickie and Mr. Cutright walked into view. Tiffany pulled her head back.

"Maybe I'm not supposed to be here right now," she thought. She decided to wait and hide until the men went away. The two men stopped on the drawbridge and looked down at the water, talking. Tiffany could easily hear them.

"This town is still sitting on the fence too much," the professor said. Mr. Cutright nodded.

"That may be so," Mr. Cutright said. "But I thought I was doing a pretty good job here. Over eighty-five per cent of the town and surrounding community is on the Point System. That's not too bad compared to the national average."

"But the Bureau wants full participation," Pickie said. "They want a hundred per cent. A few bad apples can spoil the whole barrel, as they say, and a few people not cooperating can give the others bad ideas. Like that group of Rank Blanks on the Kramar farm outside of town. A whole little town has grown up there in the last few months, and they look like they mean to stay."

"But they will have to give in sooner or later," Mr. Cutright said. "Since cash is no good, and they aren't on the Point System, they'll have to give in to buy the things they need."

"That's just the point," Professor Pickie said. "They seem to be thriving out there, and headquarters wants to know why. We think there is a black market going on or else that some in the Point System aren't loyal. They must be helping those on the farm, trading goods for labor or just giving them what they need because they feel sorry for them."

"But sooner or later they have to break," Mr. Cutright said. He tapped a cigar ash into his coffee cup and then took a big swallow.

"Headquarters isn't as convinced as you," Professor Pickie said. "You've been on the job for several months, but not everyone is on the team, and we aim to change that, one way or the other."

"You mean you want to go in and destroy the farm?" Mr. Cutright asked. "Captain Sharp has been dying to do that since the beginning of the year. He'd have plenty of support."

Professor Pickie looked at the old man with disgust. He shook his head.

"It's no wonder you haven't advanced in rank," Professor Pickie said. "All you low ranks can only think of one method to deal with a problem, and a messy method at that. With a town on the edge, if you went in with guns blazing or some such equally loud and ugly method, you'd make them martyrs. All their old friends might turn against us. You still haven't learned that the best way to eliminate a problem is to do it quietly and control it in the news and in all media. One good well-placed lie is better than a hundred bullets and much more powerful in the long run. We can eliminate this problem without firing a shot."

"How do you propose to do that?"

"You eliminate by natural causes, as they say," Professor Pickie said with a smile. "You don't need guns or bullets."

"What natural causes?"

"Have you heard of the Nega Flu?" Professor Pickie asked.

"Of course," Mr. Cutright said. "It's that flu or plague that broke out in China somewhere. And India too, wasn't it? When people get it they die very fast. They freeze up like human statues, I heard. Sounds amusing. Apparently it's not too contagious. I heard it's even broken out in a few places in this country. It strikes, then it's gone, though several hundred thousand have been killed, I hear."

"Yes, only such a flu didn't break out, it was delivered to those communities on purpose," Professor Pickie said. "General Rex himself has overseen and approved the development of the Nega Flu. It's ORDER's little way to reduce populations in a controlled way. There is a vaccination which you give to your friends. Those who aren't friendly with ORDER don't receive the vaccination. When the Nega Flu is released, a vaccinated person won't even get a sniffle, but those without the vaccination are gone in a matter of minutes. It's the perfect disease to control the herds, as the General likes to say. You can deliver it through water or gas. A plague is a sad affair, but it's much more effective than bullets or noisy methods like you propose."

"No one ever tells me anything," the old man said, but Professor Pickie could see that he was pleased. The old man smiled so his yellow teeth showed. He licked his lips as he thought. "Why didn't you tell me this sooner?"

"This has to be a delicate operation, and headquarters wanted to make sure Centerville was a proper test site," Professor Pickie replied. "It looks like everything is on schedule."

"But when do we get the ingredients?" the old man asked eagerly.

"What do you think you've been producing in your very own factory this whole time?" Professor Pickie asked. "You have all the necessary chemicals here except one, but it's readily available. In fact, I brought a few barrels with me. I have enough of the Pharmakeia solvent to turn your Traginite-Z base into a thousand barrels of Nega Flu liquid, which in gas form could cover a hundred square miles or more, if we wanted."

"You mean you want to use the Nega Flu here on the Rank Blanks out at the farm?" Mr. Cutright asked.

"ORDER wants everyone to play ball and get on line," Professor Pickie said. "When people are Number Marked on July Fourth, they will also receive an antidote to the Nega Flu, a vaccination of sorts. Once everyone has been marked and is on line, we will release the Nega Flu. That will take care of the rebels and the few strays who don't want to get in step with ORDER. It's a shame, but we just can't let these few rotten apples spoil the whole bunch, can we?"

Mr. Cutright laughed and smiled.

"We'll use a test patch," Professor Pickie said. "The best way to introduce the threat of the Nega Flu to the community is to give it to a few people first. There's a standard procedure. Let me tell you back in my office."

The two men laughed as they walked back down the drawbridge.

Tiffany looked out from behind the castle wall. She didn't understand all that she had heard, but it didn't sound good. She waited a long time. When she was sure the men were gone, she walked quickly out of the building. She got on her bike and headed toward town. She was going back down through the town square when she saw a commotion over at the west side of the square in front of the newspaper office. She saw Sloan in his Commando Patrol uniform and his friends. She rode over slowly to see what was going on. She blinked in surprise when she saw Josh Smedlowe talking on the sidewalk to Mr. Turner, the newspaper editor. John Kramar and Daniel Bayley were standing next to Josh. Tiffany rode in closer to hear what they were saying.

"Why won't you print the article I submitted, Mr. Turner?" Josh asked.

"You aren't a staff member of this paper," the man said. He was clearly bothered by having Josh question him.

"You didn't even print my information as a letter to the editor," Josh replied. "Why not even a letter?"

"Your ideas are counterproductive to the aims of the ORDER government," Mr. Turner said. "Besides, they'd shut me down if I printed something like that."

"So you're saying I have a point, but you're just afraid of the government?" Josh asked. Tiffany was surprised at how insistently Josh acted.

"You also don't have any facts to back up your story," Mr. Turner said.

"Facts?" Josh exploded. "I had a ton of facts in my report. You saw what people have said about the Nega Flu. Reliable scientists have stated that it seems to have some common elements with Traginite-Z. They've tested it."

"That's what you say," Mr. Turner replied. "I've never heard of those scientists. The ORDER government is doing everything it can to stamp out disease and hunger and pain in the whole world. You're just making wild accusations, trying to cause trouble like all Rank Blanks. You see a conspiracy or some evil behind every imaginary bush. The fact is, your group just wants to make trouble for a legitimately elected government."

"The fact is, we know they're up to no good and want to expose it, but it's hard when all the people in the media have sold out to ORDER," Josh replied.

Mr. Turner's face turned very red.

"You watch who you're accusing, sonny," the man said. "I know you want to be like your dad and be some hotshot reporter. You concoct some crazy story so you can grab a headline or two. Well, it won't work."

"You're not even listening to me," Josh countered.

"Look, kid. This is a small town with a small paper," Mr. Turner said. "I'm not going to print your so-called story. It's just a bunch of non-sense."

Sloan moved in closer and stood next to Mr. Turner. He glared at Josh.

"This rabble rouser trying to give you trouble. Mr. Turner?" Sloan asked.

"I'm just trying to get him to print a truthful story," Josh said. "But no one is interested in the truth anymore."

"The truth according to whom, big mouth?" Sloan demanded. "I think you're just causing trouble and need to get out of here right now."

"Come on, Josh," John Kramar said. "It's no use. We don't want trouble with these guys."

"I'm not afraid of him," Josh said. He turned and faced Sloan. "You guys would have made good Nazis. You were born too late."

"You were born with a big mouth," Sloan said. "And I'm going to shut it once and for all."

Sloan lunged and swung a fist straight at Josh's head. Josh stepped quickly to one side. As Sloan came forward, Josh pulled his arm and yanked. Sloan flew through the air and landed flat on his back.

"Ooooomph!" he grunted. He lay on the ground gasping for air. Tiffany thought he looked like a fish. She almost wanted to laugh, but the air was too tense.

"We better go," John Kramar said nervously. All the Commando Patrol boys looked in surprise at Josh.

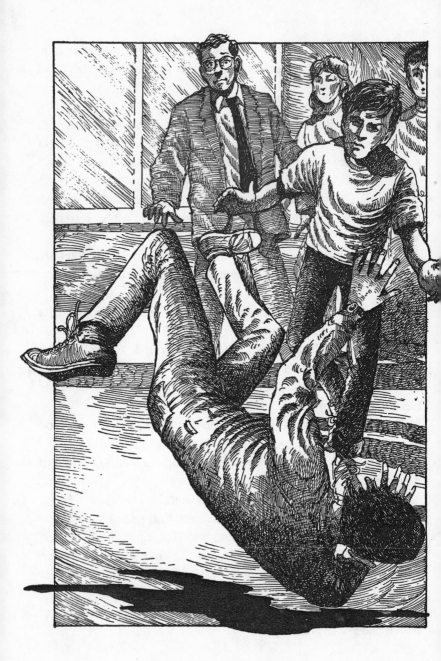

"I'm just defending myself," Josh said. "He swung at me first."

"Get him, you guys!" Sloan gasped out. But the gang of guys looked at Josh with new respect. Their hands were clenched in fists.

"Bullies are always cowards deep inside," Josh said to Sloan. Then he looked at Mr. Turner. "But they aren't the only cowards around here."

Mr. Turner looked down at the ground as Josh walked away. He and John and Daniel got on their red bikes and began to pedal away. Tiffany stared at Josh with surprise and wonder.

"Josh," she called out. She ran over to him. She wanted to hear more about this thing called the Nega Flu since she had just heard Mr. Cutright and Professor Pickie discussing the same thing.

The boys on the old red bikes stopped and looked at Tiffany. She suddenly felt embarrassed.

"I just wanted to ask . . ." Tiffany paused. "I mean, it sounds like. . . ."

"Tiffany, get away from those goons!" Sloan yelled out. All his friends were watching her talk to Josh.

"What's wrong?" Josh asked. He could clearly see that Tiffany was troubled.

"Nothing," Tiffany said. "I better go."

She walked over to Sloan and the others. Sloan was rubbing his back. He frowned at Tiffany.

"What are you talking to those morons for?" he demanded.

"I didn't say anything," Tiffany replied hotly.

"Maybe she was going to fight him," Jason called out and laughed. "I like a girl who will stick up for her older brother."

"Shut up," Sloan threatened as his face turned red.

"It was just a joke," Jason said. The other boys smiled. Tiffany turned to look back at Josh, but the boys on the old red bicycles had gone.

THE
SOUND
OF SIRENS
· · · · · · · · ·

11

The next day, on Sunday afternoon, Tiffany
heard the sound of several sirens. The siren sound always made her feel
uneasy. She was outside, planning to go see Granny Smith. She had
finally decided to ask Granny Smith some questions about the little
book. The sirens were heading north. She got out her bicycle and started
following their sound.

As Tiffany road through town, the sirens faded away as they went out
of town. Tiffany rode out to Glory Road. As she rode around the curve
heading toward the retirement home, she was surprised to see several
ambulances and police cars there.

"Someone must have gotten sick," she thought. She suddenly got a cold feeling in her stomach. She hoped that it wasn't Granny Smith. She pedaled faster.

Tiffany rode up on her bicycle, but even a block away, the home was blocked off by long yellow strips of plastic hung like rope on wooden stakes. Men in fire suits with gas masks were walking in and out of the home. Tiffany looked frantically for Granny Smith.

"What's going on?" she asked. "Was there a fire?"

"No fire," the young man said. "Some kind of problem though. Real bad they say. Someone's sick. May be some kind of gas leak or something. They want everyone to stay back until they get it under control."

"But why would they have it closed off?" Tiffany said. "What's wrong? My granny lives there. I want to go see her."

"Sorry, miss, but I have my orders. No one but authorized personnel can go beyond this line," the young man said.

"But Granny Smith lives there," Tiffany said. "She's my relative."

"Sorry, I can't let you through," he said. "It might be dangerous if there is a gas leak."

Tiffany waited anxiously and then pedaled her bicycle around the edge of the yellow taped border. No matter where she went, she still couldn't get any closer to the place. More and more people came out to see what was going on.

Sloan and his Commando Patrol came out together. They were watching the action with great interest. Tiffany rode over to him.

"Do you think you could find out what's going on?" Tiffany said. "I want to make sure Granny Smith is ok."

"She's as healthy as an old buzzard," Sloan said. "Nothing would be wrong with her. I heard they had some kind of leak or something."

Farther down the road, Tiffany saw an old red tractor chugging up to the yellow line. Right away she recognized the old man and woman whom Granny Smith had talked to before. Tiffany rode slowly toward the tractor. She wasn't sure if she would talk to the old man or not. But as it turned out, when she got close enough, he spoke to her.

"You're Tiffany Favor, aren't you? Pearl Smith's niece?" the old man on the tractor asked.

"Yes. We call her Granny Smith, but really she's my great aunt on my mom's side of the family," Tiffany said.

"She's a fine woman," the old man said . "A very fine woman. I hope she's ok. We saw an emergency bulletin on the news, and I came to see if there was anything I could do."

"Do you know what the emergency is?" Tiffany asked. "No one seems to know for sure."

"Not really," the old man said, shaking his head. His eyes were filled with concern. "Something seems different about this situation. I've seen a lot of emergencies in my day, but this is . . ."

Before the old man could finish, the sirens started to wail again. Firemen ran out of the building waving their arms. They were telling everyone to get back. All over, men were running away from the building.

"Please clear the area! Please clear the area immediately!" someone yelled on a bullhorn. People in cars started to leave in a hurry. When Tiffany saw Sloan and his friends take off on their bicycles, she was worried. Sloan usually didn't like to leave something exciting like this unless he just had to go.

"I better leave too," Tiffany shouted above the noise to the old man on the tractor. "There must be something really wrong. Maybe they think there'll be an explosion or something."

"Do you need a ride?" the old man asked.

"I've got my bike," Tiffany said. She turned and stood up on her pedals. She headed for town. More and more people in the crowd were leaving.

"Get out of here fast!" a fireman yelled at Tiffany. "This place has got to be quarantined now!"

Tiffany pedaled faster. Even the young man whom she had first spoken to was leaving in his truck.

Tiffany's stomach tightened more and more as she saw people rushing away. One car ran into the back of an old pickup and smashed the fender. But neither person stopped. They just kept going.

The tightness grew more and more inside Tiffany as she pedaled away. She felt tears coming to her eyes. All the cars rushing past her reminded her of the way people acted the night of the Halloween War. That seemed like years ago, though it had only been months. Everyone had been in a panic that night too. Now people seemed just as scared.

"What's happened to Granny Smith?" Tiffany asked herself.

She pedaled home. The town siren was blowing as she rode down Main Street. Everywhere she looked, people were locking up stores, or going inside their homes and locking the doors. Dogs howled as the sirens wailed.

Tiffany's parents weren't home. She called the office, but her father wasn't there. There was only a recording saying that the plant had been closed for emergency reasons.

Ten minutes later, her mother and father and Sloan all came home at the same time. Her father immediately locked the doors.

"Turn off the air conditioner and make sure all the windows are closed," he said. Sloan ran upstairs. Her mother walked quickly around the rooms downstairs, checking the windows.

"What's going on?" Tiffany asked. "I went out to the retirement home, but they wouldn't let me see Granny. Then everyone started running away. Was there some kind of gas leak?"

Her mother and father both came back into the hallway. Her father looked tired, and her mother's eyes were red. Tiffany knew something was very wrong. Her mother definitely looked different, as if she'd been crying, and she hardly ever cried.

"What's wrong?" Tiffany asked. "Why is everyone so scared?"

"Your father has to make some phone calls," Mrs. Favor said.

"But what about Granny Smith?"

Mr. Favor looked at Tiffany and then at his wife. He ran upstairs. She heard the door to her parents' bedroom close.

"Mom, what's going on?"

"There's been an accident," Mrs. Favor said. "Some kind of terrible accident."

"You mean a gas leak at the old people's home?" Sloan asked.

"It's a retirement home," Tiffany said. "They don't like to be called old people."

"Well, that's what they are," Sloan said. "I can't help it if they're old."

"Children, please don't fight," Mrs. Favor said.

Mr. Favor came out of the bedroom. His face was pale. He walked down the stairs slowly. Tiffany thought he was walking like an old man.

"It's worse than what we thought," he said to his wife. Mrs. Favor cried out softly and covered her mouth with her hand. She turned away from the children.

"What is it?" Tiffany asked. "What's worse than you thought?"

"Was there a gas leak at the old folks' home?" Sloan asked. He looked very interested. "Did it explode?"

"No, it's nothing like that," Mr. Favor said. "Apparently they had a new man come to stay there today. He was sick, only no one knew it. Have any of you heard of the Nega Flu?"

"The Nega Flu?" Tiffany asked. "They talk about it on television sometimes. Isn't it some bad disease over in poor countries where a lot of people get sick and die?"

Tiffany wanted to say she had heard Mr. Cutright and Mr. Pickie talking about it just yesterday. But something made her keep quiet.

"They call it the modern plague," Sloan said. "I read about it in history class right before school was out. They say it's really bad. Hundreds of thousands were killed in China. They say people get it and get stiff as a board. I saw some pictures on television. Those dead people looked just like statues. They didn't even look sick, just frozen or something."

"Well, it's not only overseas," Mr. Favor said. "There's been a few places where it's been in this part of the world and in this country. In fact, the county medical people I just talked to aren't sure, but they suspect that what happened out at the home is a result of the Nega Flu."

"What happened at the home?" Tiffany asked. "You mean that new man died?"

Her father was quiet. Mrs. Favor walked over and stood by Tiffany and hugged her.

"It's not just that man, honey," Mr. Favor said. "The Nega Flu is highly contagious. At least in confined areas. No one is sure how it spreads, but . . ."

"You mean other people got sick too?" Tiffany asked. She began to feel hot.

"All the people in the Glory Road Retirement Home have passed away, Tiffany," Mr. Favor said. "Granny Smith was with them all. They think it happened very quickly and that they didn't suffer much. But they had the classic appearance of people with Nega Flu. It's a shock to us all."

Tiffany stood still. Then she began to shake. She couldn't believe it. Her face was hot.

"You're kidding," Tiffany said. "You aren't really telling me the truth!"

"I'm sorry, honey," Mr. Favor said. "We all know how much you loved her, and how much she loved you. But she's gone now."

"Noooooooo!!" Tiffany yelled. She ran up the stairs to her room. She fell on her bed among all the stuffed animals. She cried for a few moments, but then suddenly it was over, as if a switch had been turned. Tiffany was surprised. She thought she would cry more, but she just felt cold and empty and dry.

She heard a noise behind her. Her mother was at the door. Her mother's nose was red.

"We've got to be strong, Tiffany," her mother said. "And we've got to be careful. Your father wants to talk to all of us."

Tiffany nodded. She got up and went downstairs. Her father and Sloan were sitting at the kitchen table. Tiffany walked over and sat down.

"The government is asking everyone to take precautions until we're sure this Nega Flu stuff is under control," Mr. Favor said. "It seems to come and go quickly in areas. It's a disease no one knows too much about yet. There was talk about evacuating the town, but I think they said it wouldn't be necessary."

"What about the movie?" Sloan asked. "I wanted to be a star."

"This is more important than the movie," his father said. "If it's just an isolated incident, we'll be ok. I've made several calls. ORDER and Goliath are working on a vaccine for this thing, but it hasn't quite been perfected yet. I've had Mr. Cutright make some calls to top-level officials. They all said that if it's the Nega Flu, it only seems to last twenty-four hours at the most. Some say it only lasts a few hours. It's a mystery."

"But we were out by that home when this was all going on. Do you think we got infected too?" Sloan paused. He felt his forehead. "I don't feel hot or anything."

"How do you know if you've got it?" Tiffany asked.

"Well, it's not a long illness apparently," Mr. Favor said. "You get cold because your circulation slows down. Then your heart just stops. Somehow, this disease affects something in the brain or in the autonomic nervous system. They say it's like your brain just cuts off your heart, and you die instantly after that. It's sort of like a heart attack, but the heart can be healthy. In older people, it tends to happen more quickly. The body does get very tight and stiff. The problem is that scientists don't know how it's spread. They assume the new resident who came in that morning had something to do with it. Their guess is that some people can be carriers and not actually have the disease. Or maybe it's not carried by people at all. It's too new of a problem for scientists to have figured out yet."

"What about Granny Smith?" Tiffany asked. "What will happen to her . . . her body?"

"They took them all to the capital," her father replied, "so they can be studied. In the meantime, we'll have a memorial service or something."

"She loved me so much, and I loved her," Tiffany said, beginning to sniffle. "Why did she have to die? She wasn't even sick."

"It's just one of those things, honey," her mother said. "Granny Smith was very old. She had a long life. And her Quality of Life Grade wasn't that good anymore anyway."

"None of you loved her like I did," Tiffany said. "None of you went to visit her hardly ever."

"I know she cared about you very much, " Mrs. Favor said.

Tiffany thought she would cry again, but no tears came. She thought of Josh and the Nega Flu. The more she thought, the more she tried to remember what Mr. Cutright and Professor Pickie had been saying. They seemed to know about the Nega Flu and an antidote, they said. Tiffany felt more and more confused.

The Favors stayed inside with all the doors and windows shut tightly until bedtime. The air conditioner was off and the house got warm. Tiffany went to bed and had a terrible dream. In the dream, she was running through the streets of Centerville. It was filled with human statues, only they were real people, killed by the Nega Flu. She woke up twice and went downstairs to get a drink of cool water from the refrigerator. It seemed as if morning would never come.

PETER AND POLLY

• • • • • • • •

12

Tiffany woke up on Monday morning with a cold, empty feeling. She still couldn't believe that Granny Smith was gone. Her father said it was safe to go outside. Sloan couldn't wait to gather the guys in his Commando Patrol to talk about the recent events. When Tiffany asked if she could come along, he said it would be ok. She rode her bicycle behind his all the way to the town square. In a few minutes, several of the guys in the Commando Patrol appeared.

They were all together in the middle of the town square on the sidewalk near the old wooden gazebo. Sloan swaggered across the lawn to the drinking fountain as if daring the other guys in the Commando

Patrol. They were very willing to let Sloan drink first. Then, reluctantly, they took their turns. Sloan wiped his mouth and looked around the town square.

"This place will really be something when the movie guys start filming," Sloan said. "And when everyone gets Number Marked, things will go a lot smoother. I was talking to Captain Sharp, and he thinks the Big Board will be operating at full capacity then. He said there could be big responsibilities for me after that. But I told him that I might have to take some time off leading the Patrol and all once the filming starts."

"What did he say?" Jason Miller asked.

"He understood," Sloan said, throwing his leg lazily over the seat of his Goliath Super Wings. "Once I get the part, I don't know how much time I'll have. Professor Pickie said making a movie is a lot more work than it appears. It takes a lot of time to set up the scenes and do things more than once. They may be filming more than a month. Then I'll be back for other important jobs."

"I sure hope we get to be in the film," Jason said. "I'd at least like a little part."

"Maybe you could be my saddle boy in the castle scene or an armor bearer or something," Sloan said.

"You think I could be an armor bearer too?" Jeff asked. "I'd make just as good an armor bearer as Jason."

"Would not!" Jason spat out.

"Would too," Jeff said defiantly.

"You don't even know what an armor bearer is," Jason said trying to sound as superior and confident as he could.

"Neither do you," Jeff replied.

"Hey, cool down," Sloan said with a confident smile. "I can probably have two armor bearers. If I'm the star, they'll give me star treatment, right?"

The other boys smiled and nodded. They always agreed with Sloan, Tiffany thought. She wondered if they were afraid of him.

"I heard they had the Number Marking machine all set up," Jeff said.

"Yeah, I heard that, too," Sloan replied. He looked over at the court-house.

"All my friends say they are going to get Number Marked in their hands," Tiffany said. "What are you guys going to do?"

"I want to have it in my hand," Jeff said.

"Me too," Jason added.

"Not me," Sloan said. "I want it right between the eyes. I want every-one to know that I'm loyal to ORDER the second they see me."

"But you can hardly even see the mark," Tiffany said. "They say it's too tiny."

"I don't care," Sloan said, licking his lips as if he was hungry. "I want it between the eyes."

"Maybe I'll do it that way too," Jeff said.

"Me too, now that I think about it," Jason added. Sloan looked at his followers and smiled.

"Let's go out and see how the auditions are going," Jeff said.

"Yeah, maybe they'd let us try out again, just in case," Jason replied.

"I think it would be a good idea," Sloan said. "I might as well get used to hanging around there. It will be my home away from home pretty soon."

The boys and Tiffany rode out to the big warehouse on the Goliath factory grounds. No one knew for sure when Professor Pickie would announce who had what parts in the movie. But since it was the last day for auditions, everyone hoped he would give out the parts soon, maybe even that day. Lots of people were in the big warehouse. The second- and third-grade children were supposed to try out for parts of the townspeople. The boys watched for thirty minutes. Tiffany and her friends were watching too. When there was a break, everyone went outside. Tiffany wanted to talk to Mary Ann about Granny Smith's death. But everyone else wanted to talk about the movie. No one wanted to think about death, Tiffany thought. Since the immediate danger was over, everyone seemed to forget.

Soon a big white limousine pulled up into the parking lot. Tiffany and Sloan and all the others watched. The driver, a chauffeur in a black uniform, got out and hurriedly opened the back door. A tall woman got out.

"She's beautiful," Tiffany said softly. The woman wore diamond earrings and a diamond necklace on a pale blue suit. Her white-blond hair was piled high on her head. "She looks like an heiress or something."

The chauffeur continued holding the door open. All the children blinked in surprise when a boy and girl got out. Both kids wore casual, but expensive clothes. They appeared to be about the same age as their group of Centerville admirers. The girl looked over at the other children and smiled slightly. The boy cocked his head confidently as he casually appraised the crowd. He looked away without acknowledging that he even noticed the other kids.

"Wow!" Sloan said. "Look at that girl. She looks great. I haven't seen anyone that nice-looking since we left the city. She sort of looks familiar too."

"That guy's not too bad either," Mary Ann whispered. "He's an absolute hunk. I think they both look familiar. I wonder who they are, and what they're doing here."

The woman and two children followed the chauffeur into the warehouse.

"Maybe we can stay a little while longer to see what's going on," Sloan said.

"I'm game if you're game," Jason said.

All the Centerville kids rushed to get back into the warehouse. Sloan was the first inside the big metal building, followed by Tiffany and the others. They were all surprised when Professor Pickie stopped and greeted the woman, kissing her on the cheek, and then hugged the children.

"They must be his family," Sloan said.

"Wow!" Tiffany said. "He's going to live on our street too, I heard."

"Yeah, she is," Sloan said. He watched the girl look in her purse. She brought out a small mirror, checked her face, and closed it.

"They're going to live on your street?" Jason asked.

"Yeah," Sloan said. "Professor Pickie is going to be in that big new house at the end of Buckingham. It's not all the way done yet. It's even bigger than our house. But they don't have a pool."

"Not yet," Tiffany said. "But Dad said they would have a pool bigger than ours."

"Who cares?" Sloan said. He stared at the new boy cautiously.

"I wonder if he'd like to be in our Patrol," Jason said. "I bet he'd be a great member. With him in our Patrol, we'd be the best in town."

"We already are the best in town," Sloan said, suddenly irritated. "We don't need him to be the best. You've got me."

"Yeah, well, you know what I meant," Jason said.

"I wonder if she knows any movie stars?" Mary Ann asked in hopeful tones.

"I bet she does," Sharon said. "I wonder if they'll ever come visit her or come to her parties."

"How do you know they'll even have parties?" Tiffany asked.

"Well if they do, I want to be invited," Mary Ann said. "I bet they'll be great."

"We have good parties at our house!" Tiffany said defensively. "You act like you never went to a good party in your life."

"I was just saying I bet they have good parties too," Mary Ann said.

"Yeah, with movie stars and who knows who else?" Sharon added.

"I think you guys are making too big a deal about them," Tiffany said quickly. "She's probably a big snob."

Professor Pickie looked up and waved for the children to come down. Sloan walked down to the group.

"I'd like you all to meet my family," Professor Pickie said enthusiastically. "My wife's name is Pauline. This is Peter, my son who just turned thirteen. And this is Polly, my daughter. She's twelve like you, Tiffany."

All the Centerville kids muttered hellos. Sloan stepped forward and stuck out his hand.

"Sloan Favor," he said. "I live just down the street from where your new home is being built."

"And this is his sister, Tiffany," Professor Pickie said. "I told you about the Favor children, remember?"

"Yeah, sure," Peter Pickie said with a confident smile. He seemed amused about something. "You guys are the competition, I hear."

"Competition?" Sloan asked.

"For the two starring roles," Polly said. She had a rich, deep voice that was vibrant and energetic. "My father says you two are the leading contenders for the roles."

"That's what everyone says," Sloan said, nodding his head up and down with a smile.

"Of course we haven't auditioned yet," Peter Pickie said. He looked at his sister with a slight smile. His arms were folded across his chest.

"You're auditioning?" Jason asked Peter. The new boy nodded. He looked with great pleasure at Sloan's face.

"For the starring part in the movie?" Sloan added.

"What other part is there except the starring role?" Peter asked as if surprised.

"Well, there're the extras and the townspeople," Jason said.

"The extras?" Peter asked as if he thought the idea was funny.

"Are you trying out for the part of the princess?" Mary Ann asked Polly.

"I thought I'd give it a try," Polly said energetically. She had a strong smile and beautiful teeth. Tiffany took a deep breath as she looked at her. "Of course, I've only worked in television before. I've never been in a movie."

"You were on television?" Sharon asked, suddenly impressed. "I knew I'd seen you before. What show was it?"

"I was on the sitcom *The Kids Are Wild*," Polly said.

"I saw that!" Mary Ann said. "And Peter was one of the guys, right? You were the baseball star in the show, right?"

Peter Pickie smiled and nodded.

"I remember that show," Sloan said. "Didn't it get canceled?"

"The old ratings war," Polly said, nodding her head. "That's show biz, as they say. But there's no business like it."

"Yeah," Tiffany said slowly. "So you have a lot of experience. You even got to sing on that show."

"I like singing, " Polly said. "We may even put a song or two in *The Mark of Perfection,* Daddy says."

"Really?" Tiffany asked. She suddenly wished she had taken the singing lessons her mother had suggested.

"You kids better go to the wardrobe room and get your costumes on," Professor Pickie said. "I want to get your tests in today."

"Nice to meet you," Polly said, waving. She followed her mother off stage. Peter Pickie smiled slightly and also walked toward the costume room.

"She's really cute, don't you think?" Mary Ann asked.

"I knew I had seen her before," Sharon added. "I didn't really like that show that much, but hey, that's Hollywood. They have actual acting experience."

"But not movie experience," Sloan insisted a little too quickly. Tiny beads of sweat glistened on his upper lip. His eyes were stormy. "They said they'd never been in a movie."

"But they've been on television!" Jason said. "It sounds like you have some real competition after all."

Soon Peter and Polly emerged in their costumes. The kids watched the pair from behind the big hot lights.

"He makes you really think he is a prince, doesn't he?" Jason said.

"I think so," Mary Ann said softly. Her eyes were filled with admiration.

Sloan just watched silently. He laced and unlaced his fingers nervously. The storm in his eyes only seemed to be growing.

"And cut!" Professor Pickie said loudly. "Good job, Peter. You missed your mark on the bridge, though. You walked too far."

"I wanted to be closer to the camera," Peter said, adjusting his royal costume. He put his sword in the scabbard on his side. "I think you should make the dragon fight longer too. Let it build more, and make the prince seem to be in real trouble. Maybe he could fall down and then get up and struggle more before killing the dragon. Don't make it look too easy."

"I thought of that," Sloan said softly.

"Did you tell Professor Pickie?" Jason asked.

"No," Sloan said angrily. "But I thought that same thing, letting the prince fall down and then kill the dragon."

"Sure you did," Jason said, as if he didn't believe him.

"I did!" Sloan insisted. "I was just going to bring it up later when I was playing the part."

"She looks like a real princess," Mary Ann said in hushed tones.

"A regular queen," Susan said. "She looks like she was born to play that part."

"Oh, sure!" Tiffany steamed. "No one is born to play anything. I can't believe you guys!"

"You sound worried," Mary Ann said, smiling. "Maybe you'll have to get a role as an extra, just like the rest of us."

Tiffany didn't say anything. Like the others, she watched quietly as Peter and Polly Pickie waltzed through their auditions. The starring role that she had assumed would be hers soon seemed to be as distant as last week's dreams.

FUNERAL
HOME

· · · · · · · ·

13

Tiffany woke up the next day feeling like life was over. There was going to be a memorial service for Granny Smith that day. The auditions were over, though starring roles hadn't been announced. But all the kids agreed that Polly and Peter Pickie were the new leaders in the race for stardom. Tiffany couldn't believe that things could change so quickly. There was hardly time to think since the memorial service was at ten in the morning.

She dreaded going to the funeral home. Her mother made her wear a dark blue dress since she didn't have any black clothes. Her whole family filed into the home slowly. As soon as she was inside,

Tiffany wanted to get out since the place seemed creepy and gloomy. Even though there wasn't a casket for her Granny Smith, Tiffany saw a casket in another room. She just hoped the whole thing would be over quickly.

She had never been to a funeral before and didn't really know what to expect. The room seemed to be covered in shadows, as if the light bulbs weren't powerful enough to be bright. There were no windows. Everyone was dressed in dark, serious clothes. And though there were flowers at the front of the room, they weren't happy flowers, she thought. Death flowers.

"Why did Granny Smith have to die now?" Tiffany thought as she followed her family up to the front of the room. "Why did she have to die at all?"

Tiffany sat down in the front row which was a long padded pew. The flowers were only ten feet away. She could smell the large, sad arrangement, and the smell wasn't a happy perfume, but a heavy, sober aroma.

"Sit up straight," Mrs. Favor said. Tiffany sighed and did as she was told.

"When will this be over?" she muttered. Her mother didn't act like she heard her. Sloan sat on the other side of her father. He sat up straight and erect in his dark blue suit. He looked alertly around the room, at the people who were arriving. He waved to one of his friends. Sloan seemed to be having a good time. But he always has a good time, Tiffany thought.

Tiffany still couldn't believe that Granny Smith was gone. She knew that death was supposed to happen eventually, but she had never really thought Granny would actually die. No one close to Tiffany had ever died before. She didn't know what to think. She had just felt a kind of numbness and cold inside. Tiffany stared at the sad flowers thinking of her Granny Smith's smile. She couldn't believe that she would never talk to her again.

"You always think things will just keep going on and on the same," she thought. "You take people for granted and never know how much you'll miss them until they're gone." Death seemed so suddenly harsh and final. But Granny Smith had never acted worried about dying. The last time she had talked to her, Granny had said that when you died you went to live with the Three Kings and that it would be exciting and wonderful. Tiffany wondered if it were true. She wished it were true, but she just wasn't sure what to believe or what to think about the kings. Tiffany still had so many questions to ask.

"I want to know what's true, and if you're true," Tiffany said deep inside herself. "Tell me if you're really true, tell me Granny Smith is ok. Tell me I'll see her again and we'll still be friends . . ."

Tiffany put her face down in her hands. Nothing seemed so exciting and wonderful about being left behind. Her life seemed to have a great big sad and vacant hole in it with Granny Smith gone. Tiffany felt as if she would miss Granny forever and ever, and that was too hard to think about.

Some of Granny Smith's friends stood up and talked about what a good person she was, but Tiffany barely listened. None of them could describe the Granny she knew, how she was always kind and full of smiles and hugs.

"She always listened to me and didn't act busy," Tiffany thought. "No one else really cared about what I have to say or think. But Granny did."

Tiffany looked at the flowers again, trying not to cry. She was afraid she would howl out in loneliness and anger if it didn't get over soon. She clenched her fists and felt her whole body go tight and stiff with feelings that she didn't understand.

"Why did Granny leave me?" was all the girl could think. "Why did she have to go away now?"

When it was over, Tiffany took a deep gulp of air once she got outside. The sky was very dark and cloudy, but it still seemed lighter than inside the funeral home. Without a word, she turned and walked quickly to their black car. She got in the back seat and waited. A few moments later her mother and father came out to the car.

"Tiffany, you're crying," her mother said. The heavy car doors shut. Sloan looked at his sister curiously.

Tiffany hadn't realized there were tears coming down her face. She wiped her eyes with her hand.

"Where did she go, Mommy?" Tiffany asked, her voice cracking. "What happened to Granny? Why did she leave me? I needed her."

Suddenly, she didn't feel numb any longer, but terribly sad and afraid and alone. She began to cry harder. The bad feelings just seemed to get worse. Her father started the car and drove toward home as Tiffany sniffled in the back seat.

"What happened to her?" Tiffany demanded.

"She died, dummy. What do you think?" Sloan answered.

"Sloan, don't be so insensitive," Mrs. Favor said. "Tiffany was very close to Granny. It's ok, honey. It was just her time to go."

"Go where?" Tiffany asked. "Everyone acts like it's so natural, but where did she go? What happens when you die?"

"Tiffy, that's just one of those big, hard-to-answer questions about life," Mr. Favor said. He reached into the back seat and patted Tiffany's knee. "You're much too young to be worrying your pretty head about death and all those kinds of questions. The important thing is to live your life to the fullest. We'll all miss her. But she was sick and old and tired. Her Quality of Life Grade was very low, actually. All those people out at the home had lived full lives. They say people that get the Nega Flu die peacefully."

The car turned slowly onto Buckingham Street. Mr. Favor pulled into the driveway. The garage door went up automatically and the car rolled inside.

"Let's all go inside and have something cool to drink," Mrs. Favor said. "We can change into some comfortable clothes. Maybe we'll find out who got the starring roles in the movie. I heard there was some stiff competition."

"Yeah," Sloan grunted. His face brightened. "But I don't have to give up yet."

He ran into the house. A few minutes later he was wearing his gray Commando uniform. He hopped on his Goliath Super Wings and rode down to the town square. He parked by the old courthouse and strode inside. Captain Sharp was talking to some men inside by the front desk.

"I'd like to get Number Marked today, sir," Sloan said, trying to sound as businesslike as possible.

"You want to be the first one, eh?" Captain Sharp asked.

"Yessir," Sloan said. "I know it's important in the movie, and I thought that if I was marked before the filming, it might help me be more prepared for the starring role, if I get the role, that is."

"I see," Captain Sharp said with a smile. "You'd like to be more prepared even than young Peter Pickie, wouldn't you?"

"A good ORDER Commando is always as prepared as possible, sir," Sloan said.

"Well, I suppose you are ready," Captain Sharp said. "I like a boy with your kind of drive. Follow me."

Sloan followed Captain Sharp into the next room. They were right under the tall, domed ceiling. A large black box, ten feet tall, stood in the middle of the room.

"You are a determined young man," Captain Sharp said. "Open the door to the Number Marking unit."

Sloan opened the door. Inside it looked darker than anything he'd ever seen. Suddenly, a round circle with an X inside lit up in dim purple light.

"Walk toward the X, my boy," Captain Sharp said from outside the box. Sloan took a deep breath and did as he was told. "Now place your right hand on the X if you want your hand marked."

"I want it right between the eyes—on my forehead," Sloan said with determination.

"You are eager, aren't you?" Captain Sharp said. "Then place your head on the center of the X."

Sloan put his head on the X, and as soon as he did, he felt the strangest sensation in his body. He felt as if he were falling and fainting, but he wasn't sure. A loud screeching noise filled his ears. He opened his eyes and for an instant he thought he saw a large black snake. Then he saw the most handsome and beautiful face he had ever seen. Part of the face reminded him of the famous General Rex, but it was as if there were a face behind a face in this man. The face glowed in purple light.

"You will swear your undying loyalty forever to my throne, won't you?" the voice asked. Sloan felt weak all over. No one, he thought, could resist such a voice. Something about that face made Sloan want to please it. Sloan felt as if he had always known this man, as if he were even Sloan's true father somehow.

"I am your father in spirit," the face said, reading Sloan's thoughts perfectly. "And I will fill you with my power and my destiny. Together we will resist every effort of those worthless kings to encroach on my throne."

"Yes, your majesty," Sloan said. "I will obey you."

The face smiled, and Sloan felt totally accepted and taken in. A humming sound filled his ears, and he felt as though his body was under great pressure—as if he was far down under water. For a moment he felt as if he couldn't breathe and he gasped. A flash of intense pain shot through him. He cried out. Then it was over. He opened his eyes and he was in the box, staring at the large circled X.

"You've been successfully Number Marked," Captain Sharp said. "You've made history, my boy. You're the first person in town to be so marked."

"Let me see," Sloan said eagerly. He walked over to a mirror. A spot of blood was on his forehead. He wiped it away. A tiny mark, about the size of a mole, was all he could see. It looked like a small tattooed scar. Sloan squinted.

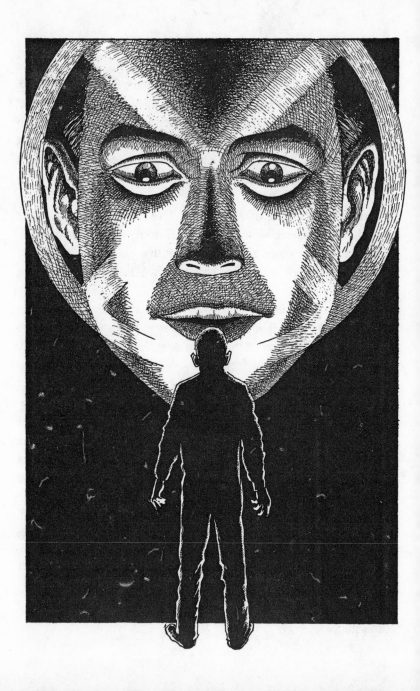

"That's odd. It sort of looks like little number sixes," Sloan said.

"That's the way they all look," Captain Sharp said. "It's the number of man. To man, by man, for man. It's a glorious new age about to start. Soon everyone will have those marks. You should be proud, my boy, to be the first in this town. When you stand in front of the Number Mark scanner, it will perform any transactions that the old number card performed. In the scanning light you will see the circled X. It's embedded into your skin."

"Wow, that's cool!" Sloan said. "I should be points ahead for sure now that I was the first one marked, shouldn't I?"

"Undoubtedly," said Captain Sharp.

"You think I'll have more points than that new kid, Peter Pickie?"

"I don't know," Captain Sharp replied, as if he wasn't really interested. "The only way to tell is to get the ranking function working again on the Point System. It's possible, I suppose."

"But I got Number Marked," Sloan said. "I'm the first in town to have it done, like you said."

"Yes, but Peter Pickie and his sister already have been Number Marked," Captain Sharp said. "They did it several weeks ago, according to the professor."

"But I thought . . ."

Sloan's face fell. He frowned. Suddenly he kicked the wall as hard as he could. He yelled out in pain.

"Kicking walls won't increase your totals, that's for sure," Captain Sharp said. "Just be glad you're marked. That way I'm sure you'll still be in the running for that very important part."

"There must be a way to outdo that guy," Sloan muttered. He walked silently out of the building. Captain Sharp began to laugh as soon as the boy was gone.

EXTRA CREDIT

· · · · · · · · ·

14

July first came, and there was still no announcement about the starring roles for the big movie. All day long the kids waited. No one had seen Professor Pickie. Sloan and Tiffany both wondered what the news would be. Sloan came home just before supper. He seemed excited, but he wouldn't tell Tiffany his secret.

Later, when his parents were gone, Sloan walked into the living room. He smiled. "We still have a chance," Sloan said. "I talked to Mr. Cutright today. He said that we are still in the running, and that's why they haven't decided. He also said we can get extra credit."

"Extra credit?" Tiffany asked. "You mean we audition again?"

"It's something like that, I suppose," Sloan said. "All I know is that it's a secret. We're supposed to go out to the warehouse at eleven tonight. No one is supposed to know we're gone, not even Mom and Dad."

"Really?" Tiffany asked. She was interested, but she wondered if the whole thing wasn't one of Sloan's schemes.

"Just be ready tonight."

Tiffany and Sloan waited until a quarter to eleven that night. They went outside quietly. The strange star shone even more brightly than just a few days before. All the other stars seemed dim. They had left their bikes around the side of the house so they wouldn't make any noise in the garage. Soon they were riding down the streets of Centerville, heading for the Goliath factory. They arrived at the big warehouse stage just before eleven.

"I don't know if this is a good idea," Tiffany whispered to Sloan as they entered the huge warehouse. "Are you sure he said to come down here this late at night?"

"That's what he said," Sloan replied. "Don't be such a baby. If you hadn't been such a klutz, I bet we would have won those roles for sure. At least we still have a chance. That's what he said on the phone."

"But why do we have to come down so late at night?"

"I don't know," Sloan said. "You know these Hollywood types. They're kind of strange."

"Well, it sure does seem weird to me," Tiffany said. They entered the big doors that opened onto the castle set. Professor Pickie was sitting in a director's chair on the set, reading a script. Only one of the big lights was turned on, a spotlight aimed at the professor.

"Welcome, my future thespians," Professor Pickie said in a deep rich voice. "Come on down!"

"He seems in a good mood," Sloan whispered as they walked down through the big dark lights. Sloan led the way across the drawbridge. Tiffany followed. As she entered the circle of light, she felt the thrill of being a star all over again. For a moment, she thought she could hear applause and cheering. Her heart raced as she felt a wave of pleasure. The sounds of her fantasy seemed so real, she almost started to bow to accept the adoration. But the instant she turned to face the audience, she realized it wasn't true. She felt embarrassed and hoped Professor Pickie and Sloan hadn't noticed her actions.

"I've got to get ahold of myself," she thought. Sloan was looking out into the darkness behind the lights.

"It's almost like I could hear them applauding," Sloan said. "Only they sound far away."

The professor stared at Sloan and smiled. He looked at Tiffany in the same knowing way. He certainly seemed like someone with a secret, she thought.

"You can almost feel it and hear it, can't you, children?" Professor Pickie said. "That's the way it is once you've tasted stardom. There's nothing quite like it—the adoration of the fans, having your face on television and in the newspapers and, best of all, there on the big screen."

When he said that, a whirring sound began above them as a large screen rolled down like a big white sheet. It slipped down slowly and then hung in midair right in front of the castle wall.

"Roll it," Professor Pickie said loudly.

The lights went out and a projection light went on. Numbers counted down on the screen. Then came the title, *The Mark of Perfection*. After the title came the words, *Favor Children Auditions*. Tiffany blinked in surprise when she saw herself and Sloan acting out their roles in full costume.

"Wow!" Sloan said with pleasure as he saw himself dashing about, swinging his sword.

"The jewels and crown look lovely," Tiffany said, staring at her image.

"Not a bad audition, is it, children?" Professor Pickie said. "Very respectable. A few flaws, but very respectable, nonetheless."

Tiffany was surprised when she didn't see herself lose the crown.

"But I thought I messed that part up," Tiffany said. She stared at the film on the screen. It was like she had always imagined herself, and what she and her mother had hoped would happen.

"That's the wonder of film," Professor Pickie said. "You can always do an extra take, shoot from a new angle, and before you know it, dreams are coming true. Stars and heroes can be made in so many ways. With enough makeup and the right lighting, anyone can be beautiful. The ordinary can become outstanding."

"I didn't think I'd look as good as I do," Sloan said with pride.

"And I'm surprised I don't look more clumsy," Tiffany added.

"That's because you children have star quality," Professor Pickie said. "It's plain to see. It's all over the big screen."

The film ran out as the townspeople were bowing down and applauding their heroes. Once again, Tiffany felt the flush of pride as she sensed the adoration of the invisible audience.

"You children both have star potential, and I'd hate to see it go to waste," Professor Pickie said. "But, of course, at this point it's only potential."

"I could do it. I know I could if you only gave me the chance," Sloan burst out. Tiffany was surprised to see her brother so eager for something. Usually he was under control and cool about everything.

"As I said, you do have potential, great potential," Professor Pickie said. He stood up and looked around the set. He walked over to the drawbridge and looked down into the water. "You have potential, but. . . ."

"But what?" Sloan asked.

"Polly and Peter both have star quality too," the professor said.

"Oh, yeah," Sloan said. "I almost forgot about them."

"I didn't," Tiffany said. "She's really pretty and great. I know she's better than I am. She seems so professional."

"She is professional," the professor said. "They both have experience and talent. They both had a great audition. The Goliath executive producers like them very much in these roles."

"I don't guess we have a chance," Tiffany said.

"Well, that's why I invited you children here," the professor said slowly. "There is a long-standing tradition in the movie industry that there are ways to get a part or a role even when you're not the first choice."

"Really?" Tiffany asked. "But how?"

"You could call it different things, but you might think of it as extra credit," the professor said.

"You mean like in school?" Sloan asked.

"Exactly," Professor Pickie said. "When your grades are low, the teacher can give you an extra project to do or another test or some such thing, and if you do well, you boost your point total."

"I've always had straight A's," Sloan said confidently.

"I have too," Tiffany added quickly. "Well, until this last quarter."

"I know how capable you children are," Professor Pickie said. "And as I said, I believe you have potential. And with a little extra credit points, I may be able to convince the Goliath producers that you would be right for the job."

"Really?" Sloan asked. "But what about Peter and Polly?"

"Well, they are professionals, as you know, and this isn't the only role they have auditioned for at this time," Professor Pickie said. "Before they came here, they were both trying out for roles in Hollywood. Now, it may be better for their careers to take those roles. Or it may be that Goliath would like truly unknown actors and actresses to be a part of this film. Or perhaps I can convince them of your qualifications if you demonstrate true star quality."

"Do you want us to do another audition?" Tiffany asked. "I bet I could do a better job. I know my mother thinks I could do better."

"I am thinking of another audition of sorts," he said. "Something that would give you extra credit and prove how valuable and loyal you are to Goliath Industries and to ORDER, the chief sponsor of this film."

"We'll do it," Sloan said quickly. "We'll do anything."

"I'm willing to do another audition for sure," Tiffany said with a smile.

"I thought I could count on you children for your cooperation," Professor Pickie said. "I have a very special, but very secret kind of audition I want you to do."

"Secret?" Tiffany asked.

"Very secret, but very vital," the Professor said. "And it needs to be done tonight."

"Tonight?" Sloan responded. "You want us to audition tonight? Shouldn't we practice and rehearse some, I mean, so we can do our best?"

"I don't mean audition on the stage," Professor Pickie said. "I have another kind of audition in mind altogether."

"What do you mean?" Tiffany asked.

"Follow me," the professor said. He walked across the drawbridge. He walked through the lights and kept on walking. He went out of the big warehouse and over to the factory. Sloan and Tiffany almost had to run to keep up with his fast steps.

Professor Pickie went into the main Goliath factory building. He walked down several halls, and then opened an office door and went inside.

"This is Mr. Cutright's office," Tiffany said with surprise.

"I wonder what he wants here," Sloan replied.

Inside, Mr. Cutright was sitting at his desk, smoking a cigar. He smiled, showing his yellow teeth, as the children came inside. In the corner were two Goliath UltraFlight bicycles. On the back of each bicycle was a small platform. Stainless steel cylinders that looked like fire extinguishers were attached to the platforms.

"I have some future stars here, I do believe," Professor Pickie announced. "They said they were willing to work for a little extra credit."

"Wonderful," Mr. Cutright said. "I knew you could count on Ken Favor's kids. They're cooperative and smart and good-looking besides. Let's get started."

Mr. Cutright stood up and walked over to the bikes. He patted the sleek seat of one of the UltraFlights.

"Are you going to film us as we ride the bikes?" Sloan asked.

"Yes, we are," Professor Pickie said. "But first you need to run a little errand for us."

"Sure," Sloan said. "What do we need to do?"

"You children are probably aware of the Kramar farm west of town out on Glory Road," Mr. Cutright said. "Since early spring, all sorts of Rank Blanks and malcontents have been gathering at that farm. They've got tents and shacks and trailers and all sorts of things out there, and it's becoming a health hazard. With this recent outbreak of Nega Flu, we're afraid that farm, with the unsanitary conditions, may be the next place the Nega Flu strikes. We're especially concerned about their water supply. The whole farm is getting water from one well. That's what makes it especially dangerous if their water system gets exposed to the Nega Flu. We have an effective treatment, if we get there in time, to prevent any outbreaks. We want you children to go out there on these UltraFlights and spray the contents of these fire extinguishers into the well. Since this is a strong chemical, you'll want to be sure to wear rubber gloves as you spray the well. I have the gloves right here."

Mr. Cutright got two pairs of big yellow rubber gloves off his desk and placed them on the seats of the UltraFlights. Tiffany stared at the bicycles.

"You want us to put something into their water?" she asked. "This late at night?"

"I know it does seem kind of secretive," Mr. Cutright said. "But these Rank Blank people have been awfully suspicious and even hostile to Goliath workers who have gone out there and offered to help treat their water. We decided we just needed to take matters into our own hands."

"But why do you want us?" Tiffany asked, frowning. Something about the whole situation made her feel uneasy inside.

"We need human children, I mean, children such as yourselves, because no one is suspicious of you," Mr. Cutright said. "Professor Pickie assured me you children were eager to take on some extra credit. Is that true or not?"

"Sure, it's true," Sloan said. "We'll be glad to deliver this stuff, and then we'll come back and do the next audition, right?"

"That's right," Professor Pickie said with a big smile.

"But why do it at night?" Tiffany insisted. She thought of Josh's warnings about ORDER and about what she had overheard. "That doesn't sound like it has anything to do with filming."

Mr. Cutright suddenly didn't look so friendly anymore as he stared at Tiffany. He chomped down on his cigar and walked slowly back over to his desk.

"Maybe these children aren't ready to be stars yet after all," Mr. Cutright said.

"Of course we are!" Sloan blurted out. He smiled at both men, pulling Tiffany's arm, dragging her toward the door.

"You're hurting my arm," Tiffany whispered.

"You want to ruin our last chance?" Sloan hissed. "You don't question a man like Mr. Cutright. You just do what he says, just like Dad always does, because he's the boss."

"But this whole thing sounds funny to me," Tiffany whispered.

"It won't be funny if we miss out on this part," Sloan insisted. "And it's for a good cause. Now quit making waves, and let's do it."

"Are you sure it's the right thing?" Tiffany asked.

"If it gets us the starring roles, anything is the right thing," Sloan said. He looked up at the two men and smiled his old, reliable smile. "My sister and I will be glad to help you out. She's just a little nervous about going out so close to those Rank Blanks since they're enemies of ORDER and all. We wouldn't be in any real danger, would we?"

"Of course not," Mr. Cutright said. He seemed reassured. "They're misguided and misdirected, confused people, but they are rather harmless, especially at night. And of course, you'll be flying in on the Ultra-

Flights. The whole operation won't take more than twenty minutes."

"We get to fly there too?" Sloan asked. His smile became genuine.

"First class all the way for our future stars," Professor Pickie said. "Now let me tell you the exact location of the well and what to do."

Tiffany and Sloan listened carefully to the instructions. The whole plan seemed simple enough. When the men were done talking, Mr. Cutright opened his big office window. He took two tubes of Wildbird Drops out of his pocket. The TRAG-Ultra7 units sucked them in.

"Off you go," he said, waving his arm.

"You mean out the window?" Sloan asked.

"Why not?" Mr. Cutright said with a smile, showing his old yellow teeth. Both children got on the sleek bicycles. Sloan was the first to pedal. The UltraFlight lifted into the air. With a shout and a whoop, Sloan shot through the open window. Tiffany followed, though going much slower.

The two men looked out the window, watching the children flying over the factory buildings.

"In a few hours, the biggest Rank Blank problem in this county will be solved once and for all," Mr. Cutright said.

"A bold move, a bold, but smart move," Professor Pickie said. "I wish we could film them when it hits."

"I think you should," Mr. Cutright said. "I'm sure you could use it in the film. The troublemakers have caused enough problems. But they could be useful in the end."

"Yes, we need several extras to play dead," Professor Pickie said. "They should be doing that rather nicely indeed."

The two men laughed together as they watched the two children fly off into the night sky, swallowed by the darkness.

AT THE
WELL
· · · · · · · ·
15

Tiffany's Ultra Flight was wobbling badly as it flew through the July sky. She held on so tightly that her hands were soon hurting from the pressure. Sloan pedaled as fast as he could, but the bike didn't seem to increase in speed.

"This bike isn't going right," Sloan said, puffing as he flew. Tiffany pedaled faster than she wanted just to keep up with her brother.

"My bike is so shaky," Tiffany said. "I feel like it's just going to fall out of the sky any minute." She looked above at the star that also seemed about to fall out of the sky. She shivered.

She looked down below. The moonlight and starlight shining on the dark treetops made her feel uneasy. Looking back toward town, she wished she was pedaling toward all the lights instead of going away from·them, out into the country. Off in the distance there were lights shining on farms, here and there. And way in the distance she could see the glow of the lights from the town of Kirksville. But that was far away. Out in the country, the darkness just seemed to be growing.

"Are you sure you'll recognize the Kramar place?" Sloan asked. "I mean, we'll be in trouble if we go to the wrong farm. I don't want to lose this role because you made a mistake."

"Stop yelling at me, Sloan," Tiffany said irritably.

"I'm not yelling."

"But you assume I'm going to mess up before we even start," Tiffany said. "You always assume you can do everything better than I can just because you're older."

"Well, it's true," Sloan said in his confident tone. "Only I've never been to the Kramar farm and you have, that's all. A person could get lost out here, it's so dark."

Tiffany didn't say anything else. She gripped the handlebars tighter and kept pedaling. She stared at the moon, and then she stared at the star. Part of her wanted to look away, but there it was like an anchor in the sky. But what did it anchor? When she looked at it, she felt doomed by the certainty of its coming. She remembered what she had read in *The Book of the Kings* about the star being a sign of the end of an era.

"What do you think that star means?" Tiffany asked.

"How should I know?" Sloan said. "No one knows for sure. They just know it's coming in this direction. I think it will burn up before it gets too close to the earth."

"You don't think it will burn us up?"

"Of course not," Sloan said. "You just can't end a planet like that."

"But doesn't that happen in outer space?" Tiffany said. "Our science teacher says lots of planets and stars and even whole galaxies have died or exploded."

"Yeah, but that won't happen to us," Sloan said, though he didn't sound too certain.

"Why couldn't it happen to us?" Tiffany asked. "It's like our planet is in the highway when a big truck comes along and pow! Remember Shemp?"

Shemp was a dog the Favors had owned three years before that had been hit by a truck in the highway. He was the only dog the Favors had ever owned. Tiffany still mourned sometimes, thinking about his death.

"The earth is a planet, not a dog," Sloan said. "It's big. Besides, the government will do something to avoid any trouble. Maybe they can bomb the star or send a spaceship up. They'll do something if there is any real danger."

"But some people think that star is bigger than our whole solar system," Tiffany said. "You couldn't blow it up with any bomb. That's just nonsense, Sloan."

"Well, I don't know what they'll do exactly," Sloan said irritably. "All I know is that if there's danger they'll do something."

"It makes me think about the kings," Tiffany said. "In *The Book of the Kings*, it says they hold the stars in their hands. It makes it sound like the stars are nothing more than a baseball to them. I bet they could make that star move off course. I bet they could knock it with their fists and it would explode."

"You've been reading that book?" Sloan asked.

"Granny Smith gave it to me right before she died," Tiffany said. "It's not like I expected. You ought to read it. It makes more sense than I thought it would. And I get this *feeling* when I read it. It's hard to describe. It makes you wonder about stuff. It makes you wonder if they know more about that star than you think. Maybe Josh is right. . . ."

"Now you're talking pure nonsense," Sloan grunted. "*The Book of the Kings* is a bunch of fairy tales for people who can't face life as it really is."

When they found Glory Road, Tiffany insisted on flying lower, just above the treetops. "I want to be closer to the ground in case this bike runs out of power," she said.

"It's not going to run out," Sloan replied. "He gave us a huge tube of Wildbird Drops. And we have extra tubes besides."

"I don't care," Tiffany said. Her stomach felt tight as a knot. "I want to fly lower. If you want to fly up high, go ahead."

"Ok," Sloan said. His tone of voice said that he felt as if Tiffany was acting like a baby.

"There's the farm," Tiffany said, pointing out in front of her. Everything looked so much different at night. Before it had seem so joyous and peaceful, and now it looked lonely and closed up. A few lights were on in windows. A light was on at the telephone pole at the end of the driveway. Another shone by the hayloft on the barn.

"There's the barn," Tiffany said. "The well is behind it."

"Let's go," Sloan whispered. "Keep quiet."

They pedaled away from Glory Road across the driveway and field of corn in front of the house. They flew quietly over the white house toward the barn. But as they got closer, both UltraFlights began to wobble.

"Something's wrong with this bike," Tiffany whispered.

"Mine too," Sloan said. He seemed surprised that the UltraFlight was shaking so violently.

"We've got to land," Tiffany said.

"Let's go further," Sloan replied, pedaling as fast as he could.

Then without warning, the wheels on both bikes locked, as if someone was pushing the brakes. They dropped rapidly. Tiffany screamed as they fell. She was sure they were going to break their necks. The bikes hit a huge pile of weeds and stopped.

"We're in a pile of hay," Sloan sputtered, spitting the hay out of his mouth.

"That was close," Tiffany said. "I don't like this. Let's get out of here."

"We're on a mission," Sloan said. "And I aim to finish it. Come on. We can still spray this stuff in the well and get out of here."

Not too far away, a dog barked. Both children froze in the moonlight, listening. The dog barked once more and then stopped.

"You think anyone knows we're here?" Tiffany whispered.

"How could they?" Sloan asked. "That dog must have heard you scream."

"I couldn't help it, Sloan," Tiffany said. Suddenly she felt like crying. She was scared, and it was dark, and something about the whole plan seemed very wrong to her. The more she thought about it, the less she trusted Mr. Cutright and Professor Pickie. The hay was sticking in her clothes and made her itch.

"Let's get it over with," Sloan said. "The barn is right over there."

Sloan stood up and unfastened the fire extinguisher from his Ultra-Flight. Then he unfastened the fire extinguisher from Tiffany's bike. He handed the heavy stainless steel cylinder to her.

"Let's go," Sloan said. He began carrying the extinguisher toward the barn. Tiffany struggled out of the hay after him. The fire extinguisher was heavy and grew heavier with each step. They passed the corner of the barn and headed toward the back.

"Sloan, I don't think we should do this," Tiffany whispered. "I'm getting a bad feeling, like something is terribly wrong."

"Pipe down, you loudmouth," Sloan hissed. "You want to wake everyone up?"

"I just think something's wrong," Tiffany insisted. She stopped and set the heavy canister down. She gulped in air to catch her breath. Sloan glared at her in the moonlight and stopped. He set down his fire extinguisher.

"I'll squirt it in the well if you're chicken," Sloan said. "Just help out. You carry your extinguisher, and I'll carry mine."

Sloan grabbed the shiny cylinder and started walking again. Tiffany sighed, picked up her fire extinguisher and followed. They had to walk around a big farm truck at the back of the barn.

"There it is," Sloan said, pointing to the well. The circular well was made of white stones and had a wooden cover over it. A small peaked, shingled roof was held up by two posts. A small pump was next to the well. A pipe connected to the pump went up and down inside the well. Sloan set down the fire extinguisher. He walked over closer to the well. He looked at the well cover, reached down and lifted. A hinged part of the cover flipped open.

"Great," Sloan said.

As Sloan turned to get his fire extinguisher, a little dog darted out from around the barn, barking as loudly as possible.

"Sssshhhh!" Sloan said, as the dog lunged forward.

"Get back, you stupid dog," Sloan said, kicking at it. The dog, a small terrier mixed with mutt, leaped back out of range. Sloan lost his balance, and the fire extinguisher dropped to the ground. The dog leaped forward, still barking.

"Let's get out of here," Tiffany said. A light went on in the house.

"Not yet," Sloan said, frowning at the dog. The little mutt ran forward as Sloan picked up the fire extinguisher. He barked and growled and came close to the boy's pant leg. In anger, Sloan turned and aimed the nozzle of the fire extinguisher at the dog. When he barked and came closer, Sloan pulled the trigger. A stream of dark liquid shot out and hit the dog in the mouth. The dog immediately stopped barking. It seemed to cough and gag. Then it was suddenly still, frozen like a statue.

"Sloan, you killed it!" Tiffany said, looking with horror at the dog.

"It was going to bite me," Sloan said angrily.

The dog didn't fall over or even move. It stood frozen, its mouth still open. Tiffany stared. Then it hit her.

"It's like the Nega Flu!" she said. "That dog has all the symptoms. Look at it. It's stiff and everything."

"So what?" Sloan said nervously. "Just don't get near it. We'll empty these in the well and then get out of here."

"But this stuff is poison," Tiffany said. "I think this stuff causes the Nega Flu."

"Don't be ridiculous," Sloan said. "This is the antidote. It must just affect dogs that way."

"No, it doesn't," Tiffany said. "I saw on the TV that it kills animals too, just like it kills people. Sloan, we can't put this in the well. It could really hurt somebody."

"I want that role in the movie," Sloan said, defiantly. "We were sent out on a mission. A good soldier does what he's told to do and doesn't ask questions. Now leave me alone."

Sloan picked up the fire extinguisher and started for the well. Before he could take two steps, bright lights came on with a rush of music. Everything seemed frozen in time under their glare. Tiffany cried out as she fell to the ground.

THE
STAR

· · · · · · · · · ·

16

The lights were blinding they were so
bright. Tiffany could hardly open her eyes to look in any direction. On
the ground, she felt so weak that she couldn't stand, even though she
tried. The music was loud and strong, but it wasn't a song. The music
seemed beautiful, but Tiffany couldn't love its beauty. She felt weighted
down with ugliness, as if the beauty of the music made her own ugliness
seem more obvious. She tried to raise herself, but the light just kept
coming and coming and coming, and seemed to go right through her,
overpowering her. She felt totally helpless and exposed under the
brightness and the loud music.

"I can't . . . I can't . . . see!" Tiffany screamed out. "Sloan, help me!"

But she couldn't see Sloan. All she could see was the light. The music grew stronger. She looked up. Even the night sky seemed full of light. For a moment Tiffany was sure she could see the mysterious star, only this time it was right on top of the farm, brighter than any sun, brighter than anything she'd ever seen before. She turned her eyes away and buried her face in her hands and began to weep. She wondered if she was about to die, if she would be crushed and then burned by the star.

She cried and cried and wasn't even sure why. She felt so exposed and dirty. She knew without a doubt that whatever was in the fire extinguisher was evil and that she had been a partner with that poison.

"I'm just like those fire extinguishers too," she thought to herself. "I'm filled with poison. I'm filled with ugliness and hatred and . . ."

She cried harder, feeling the awful, shameful evil inside herself. She felt heavy with the ugliness. Through teary eyes she looked down and saw the dark chain again. She was relieved that she wasn't blind, but the chain was all she could see. Without explanation she knew that the chain had always been there whether she had seen it or not. She looked closer. This time she saw writing on each link of the chain. Stamped in the dark links were words and dates. Tiffany tried to read the words.

On one the words said, "I hate you, Mary Ann." A date from two months before was stamped beside the words, and it was as if Tiffany could suddenly see that whole scene over again. She and Mary Ann had been eating lunch, and Mary Ann had said she wasn't going to help Tiffany with her homework. Tiffany had gotten angry and lashed out at her friend and said, "I hate you, Mary Ann." Then she and Mary Ann hadn't spoken the rest of the day.

Tiffany stared. All the links of the chain had words on them. Link after link of hate and evil and ugliness. And she realized that she had made the chain herself, link by link, and that she had to wear what she had made. One end of the chain was connected to a hard metal ring around her neck, but the other end seemed to trail off into the blinding light as if it were a judgment with no end.

"Help me," Tiffany said, crying harder. The heavy dark chain filled her with fear and shame. She felt as if she were on a stage under the lights, but this time, all the world could see that she wasn't a star at all, but an ugly, hateful person locked up with a shameful chain. Tiffany tried to hide her face with her hands, but nothing could hide or cover her. The light was too bright and the music too powerful.

Then it was quiet. Tiffany was still sobbing. The light became more dim. Tiffany peeked out from behind her hands and saw him. If she hadn't already been on her knees, she would have dropped down and bowed. A man like no other she had ever seen before walked toward her. He wore a magnificent golden crown on his head and a royal white robe. He was looking right at her with the most intense eyes that Tiffany had ever seen. She felt totally exposed before him. His eyes seemed to see every hateful, shameful thing hanging on the girl.

She quickly bowed her head, feeling too awful to look at this face. Deep inside, Tiffany suddenly understood who this person was. He was the one in the book. He was standing right in front of her, and he wasn't anything like a fairy tale. If anything, he made everything else seem like shadows and wishes. Tiffany felt as if she would just melt into water and disappear into the ground before him.

"What do you want, my child?" the man asked. His voice sounded like the loud music she had heard earlier. His voice was quiet and steady, yet seemed to have the power of thunder behind it. Tiffany was afraid, but she knew she had to answer. No one could resist a question by this person.

"I don't know . . ." Tiffany squeaked out, looking down at her hands. She wiped her runny nose. "I wanted do things right. To be perfect. But all I ever do is mess things up. I can't do anything right. And I feel so ugly and full of hate and evil. I never saw how much until now. It's been here all the time, this chain on me, but I never really saw it."

"You've seen it before," he said. It wasn't a question. And Tiffany remembered the time when Josh and the others came on their Spirit Flyer bikes. And the time when she had last seen Granny Smith.

"I have seen it," Tiffany said. "I just didn't know what to do. I tried to throw it off me. All I did was give myself a headache. I feel so worthless and ugly. No one wants to help me."

Tiffany was surprised she could actually talk to this person—and even more surprised that he listened. She thought for sure he had come to kill her for trying to poison the water.

"I didn't come to kill you but to give you life," the man said as if Tiffany had spoken her thoughts. "You have a disease, a poison in you. But I have the antidote. I have life. Do you want the gift of life?"

Tiffany gulped and looked at him. He came closer. His face seemed kind, not terrible now. He also looked very sad.

"Do you want to get rid of that chain?" he asked. He stepped even closer.

The chain began to rattle and pull, jerking Tiffany across the ground. Something somewhere was trying to pull her away from this man's presence.

"I want it off me," Tiffany blurted out. "I want life. I'm sorry for making this chain. Help me, please."

The man smiled. Tiffany looked in his eyes. She knew there was something else remaining.

"And I want you to be my king too," Tiffany said. "I don't want to be the star . . . because you're the star, aren't you? You're the one that's coming. . . ."

As soon as she said the word *star,* her eyes opened even though they were already opened. Tiffany suddenly saw new surroundings. Instead of being behind the barn, she was sitting on the floor in a magnificent room. As she looked around, she realized it was a palace room, a room that belonged to a king. Tiffany opened her eyes wider in surprise, looking at the magnificent walls. In the next room she saw a huge table that was set with elegant dishes as if a feast was about to begin.

"You're the one in the book, aren't you?" Tiffany said in wonder, staring at him. "You're the Prince of Kings. You're really him."

Tiffany looked around the room again at all the richly colored walls and the windows that looked like jewels.

"You're the Prince of Kings and this is your home, isn't it?" Tiffany asked. Her heart leaped with excitement. She didn't understand how any of it was happening, but she didn't care. She had never felt so at home, even having seen it for the first time.

The Prince smiled. Tiffany looked at him, and then did what so many have done before the same Prince. She bowed from her waist until her face touched the ground. He was beside her in an instant and reached down. He lifted the chain and broke it off her like a piece of rotten thread. For a moment his face looked pained as he touched the chain. Then he tossed it away with a flick of his wrist. The chain flashed and burned up in an instant, leaving only a trace of smoke in the air. Then even the smoke was gone.

"Wow!" Tiffany whispered. The prince reached down to help her to her feet. As she reached for his hand, she saw the scar in his palm. She looked at his face. He was still smiling, and waiting. She grabbed hold of the scarred hand, and he pulled her up.

"I feel great!" Tiffany said as music filled the air. The Prince held out his arms and Tiffany ran to him, hugging him. He held her as she cried again, but this time the tears were happy ones. With the loud joyous music, she realized they were dancing around the large room. The Prince of Kings wanted to dance with her. Tiffany had never felt such love and life flowing through her. They danced to the strong music for what seemed like a long time.

As the music grew softer, the castle walls grew dimmer. Little by little they faded from view, and Tiffany found herself standing behind the barn out on the Kramar farm. She was in the middle of a large circle of men and women and children, all watching her. No one said a word.

WHOM
CAN YOU
TRUST?
· · · · · · · · ·
17

"Welcome," an old man finally said. Tiffany immediately recognized him as being the man who had been a friend of Granny Smith.

"Do you remember me, Tiffany? I'm John Kramar," the old man said.

"Yes," Tiffany said. She looked over at the well. Both fire extinguishers were sitting on the ground. Sloan was nowhere in sight. The little dog was still standing near the well, stiff and solid, his mouth open.

"We didn't want to interrupt your dance," the old man said, "but it seems like we need to have a talk. It may be rather urgent from the look of things."

Tiffany nodded. Had they seen her dance? She suddenly felt very uncomfortable. Everyone was staring at her.

"I didn't know it was poison until Sloan sprayed it at the dog," Tiffany said softly. "I really didn't know for sure anyway, though I knew we weren't doing the right thing."

"You don't need to be afraid," the old man said kindly. "We know you belong to the kings now. We just need to find out what's been going on. Why don't you come inside the house, and we'll have a cup of tea? The rest of you can go back to bed. And no one touch that dog, or those fire extinguishers. And don't use any water for anything—drinking or cooking or washing—until we give the go-ahead."

Tiffany followed Mr. Kramar into the house. John and Susan Kramar and the other little Kramar kids went inside too. She felt scared, but the kitchen in the farmhouse seemed so nice and cozy that she also felt at home right away. Susan told Tiffany that the old man was their grandfather. While the water was coming to a boil, there was a knock at the front door. Dr. Burke and his daughter, Amy, walked through the door, followed by Josh Smedlowe. They all looked serious.

"I called Dr. Burke because he is an expert in chemistry, and we want to find out what's inside those fire extinguishers," Grandfather Kramar said.

"Don't open them!" Tiffany said, jumping to her feet. "Something bad is inside them. It killed that little dog. Sloan sprayed it to keep it quiet."

"You need to tell us everything that happened," Dr. Burke said to Tiffany. "Let's sit down."

Tiffany told the whole story, about the extra credit and how they got the fire extinguisher, the ride on the UltraFlights and about meeting the Prince of Kings.

"I don't know what happened to Sloan," Tiffany said. "After the lights came on, I didn't see him anymore. I don't think he sprayed anything into the water."

"We'll check it too, to make sure," Dr. Burke said.

"That dog was a stray," Susan said. "The poor thing came around here yesterday begging for food. No one really owned it."

"It might have saved everyone's life," Dr. Burke said, "if those fire extinguishers hold what I think they do."

"We only found one of those UltraFlight bicycles outside," Susan Kramar said. "Sloan must have gotten away on the other bike."

"But how could he when those lights came?" Tiffany said. "I could hardly move. That chain felt so heavy and I was just . . . I don't know, stuck or something. I didn't really want to run away once I saw him."

The other people in the room all smiled. Grandfather Kramar patted Tiffany on the back.

"He always makes a big impression of one kind or another once you really get to see him," the old man said with a friendly smile.

"I thought I would die or something," Tiffany said. "At first I felt so unworthy and ugly. And then when he took away my chain, I never felt so free. Then we danced in that beautiful room . . . and I was back here. It's all so strange, but nice."

"The ways of the kings can be hard to understand, especially at first," Grandfather Kramar said. "But you'll learn. You went into the Deeper World."

"I read about that in *The Book of the Kings*," Tiffany said. "I thought it sounded weird when I read about it, but it was really wonderful. I've never done anything like that before in my whole life."

"That's just the beginning," Josh said with a smile. "You'll have lots of other adventures when you're with the kings."

"That's true, Tiffany," Grandfather Kramar said. "But for now, we've got to figure out what's in those fire extinguishers."

"I don't like to believe it could be true, but I think they were trying to ruin your water supply," Dr. Burke said. "I don't want to make any hasty judgments, but I can't think of anything Goliath has that would benefit your water supply. The way that dog died looked awfully suspicious, and I'm afraid very familiar."

"They said they were trying to help prevent disease," Tiffany said. The girl felt confused. Everything was happening so fast. "They said they were afraid of that Nega Flu stuff that got loose in the Glory Road Retirement Home."

"I wish that were true," Dr. Burke said. "But we won't know what their intentions were until we run the tests."

"Can we find out tonight?" Grandfather Kramar asked Dr. Burke. "It may be rather important to know."

"I can take them down to the labs right away," Dr. Burke said.

"Can I come?" Josh said.

"No, this might be dangerous," Dr. Burke replied. "But I'll let you all know the truth as soon as I can. I'm baffled by this. I know I could lose my job. But I can't keep pretending I don't see what Goliath and ORDER are trying to do."

"We better get you home," Grandfather Kramar said to Tiffany.

"I don't want to ride that horrible UltraFlight anymore," Tiffany said. "That stupid bike crashed. Something about them is all wrong."

"Why don't you let me see that other tube of fuel too?" Dr. Burke said. Tiffany nodded and took the Wildbird Drops out of her pocket. She gave the tube to Dr. Burke.

Everyone went outside and stood by the well. Dr. Burke loaded the two fire extinguishers into his car. The stray dog that had died was carefully wrapped up in a green plastic garbage bag and loaded in the car too. Tiffany looked at the bag sadly.

"I can go with you, if you want company," Josh said softly to Tiffany. He held his red Spirit Flyer bicycle by the handlebars. He stood up straighter. She smiled back at him.

"For some reason, I don't think those old bikes are so ugly now," Tiffany said. She looked at Josh's bike with interest. "I guess I can ride on the back like the day you got me out of that place. . . ."

"You could ride on the back," Susan Kramar said as she walked over, pushing an old red Spirit Flyer. "But then you could ride your own bicycle."

"My own bike?" Tiffany asked in surprise. "Isn't this one yours?"

"No," Susan said with a smile. "This bike was leaning on its kickstand right behind you when you came back from the Deeper World and the Kingson's palace. I guess you didn't notice it with so many things happening at once."

"You mean this bike is mine?" Tiffany asked. She looked down at the old red bicycle with surprise and wonder. "But how do I pay for it? I mean, what does it cost?"

"It's a gift from the kings," Josh said with a smile. "The Kingson already paid for it a long time ago. All you have to do is accept it."

"And ride it," Susan added. "A bicycle is a lot more fun if you ride it, don't you think?"

"Well, sure," Tiffany said, finally realizing the bicycle was really hers. She swung her leg over the bike and sat down on the broad seat. When she grabbed the handlebars, she suddenly thought of Granny Smith. For a moment, she saw Granny Smith's warm smile. A wave of love flooded over and through Tiffany. "Being on this bike makes me feel good. It's sort of like being with him, isn't it?"

"You bet!" Josh said. "You learn quick, don't you? I can tell you a lot more. I mean, all of us can tell you more. But the best thing is to just take a ride. Let's go. We can talk as we ride home."

"But how does it work?" Tiffany asked. Her excitement was growing.

"Follow me," Josh replied. He pedaled out across the field. Tiffany began pedaling too.

"Just push down on the handlebars, so they're kind of aimed upward," Josh called out. Then he demonstrated. The big red bicycle rose up into the air beside Tiffany. She gasped at the sight. Then she took a deep breath and aimed the handlebars upward, just as Josh had done. To her amazement, the big front tire lifted up off the ground immediately. A few seconds later the back tire lifted up and she was flying!

"Wow, it's so smooth," Tiffany said. "This is a hundred times better than those ugly UltraFlight bikes."

"Of course," Josh said with a smile. "Those are just cheap imitations.

Spirit Flyers are the real thing. Watch me go!"

He stood up on his pedals to go faster, and the big bike soared out ahead into the night sky. Tiffany began to pedal faster. Her bicycle shot forward. She hit the brakes, and the bicycle immediately slowed down. When she saw that she was safe on the old bicycle, she pedaled faster and caught up with Josh.

The Kramar farm looked tiny and distant below them. The lights twinkled in the house and in some of the tents and trailers. On the ground, Susan Kramar was waving at them. Tiffany waved back.

"This is wonderful!" she said, looking all around her. "I mean, I never knew you could feel so free and . . . I don't know how to describe it."

She looked up at the starry sky. She wondered if the old bicycle could take her as high as the stars. Nothing would surprise her. Then she saw the other star. She stared at it with wonder and awe. Josh rode over beside her. He noticed her looking at the star.

"That star is him coming back, isn't it?" Tiffany said, not really asking.

"That's what we all think," Josh replied. "I can hardly wait."

"I was scared of it," Tiffany said. "I thought I was going to lose something or that we'd all be wiped out or I would miss something really important. But really it's a wonderful event, isn't it?"

"We think so," Josh said. "In *The Book of the Kings* it says that the whole planet has been waiting and waiting for him to come. And now he's close. We aren't going to miss anything but death and disease and tears and suffering. I'll be glad when all that's gone."

They rode toward Centerville in the twilight of the starry sky. Everything was quiet.

"I will see Granny Smith again, won't I?" Tiffany burst out as she pondered the star.

"Yes, you will," Josh said. "And I'll see my parents. We'll see everyone who chose to be with the kings."

Tiffany smiled as she pedaled along in the dreamy sky. She thought of how excited her Granny Smith would be to see her, of how she'd smile. And Tiffany would run to her arms. All her family would be glad to see her. Then Tiffany frowned.

"What about those who don't choose to be with the kings?" Tiffany asked. "What will happen to them? I mean, Sloan, for instance, thinks they're not real, that they're fairy tales."

"Well, I'm not totally sure what's going to happen to everyone," Josh said softly. "But I do know that the kings give people what they choose. They don't force anyone to love them or follow them or be in their kingdom. From what I've read and know, I think people get what they choose. The kings honor free choice."

"How could anyone not choose them if they really knew?" Tiffany asked. She paused. "But Sloan doesn't know. I wish he did. I wish my parents would meet the Kingson like I did. I mean, what if the star comes and they still haven't chosen to be with him, to come to that party?"

"I know what you mean," Josh said seriously. "But you can't make a decision like that for other people. You can love them and tell them the truth. But the problem is that those in ORDER and Goliath Industries try to lie about the kings so people get confused. They don't want people in the kingdom."

"But why, if it's the truth?" Tiffany asked. Her heart was suddenly heavy as she thought about her family. "Why wouldn't they want them to know what's true? I mean, he's so wonderful and great and majestic and kind and . . . I can't even begin to describe him. Why would anyone refuse to choose him?"

"It seems so obvious, once you've decided for yourself, doesn't it?" Josh said. "But look at yourself. A few hours ago, you didn't really know him. But then you had the chance, and you took it. But deep down in your heart, you had been asking to know him and to know what's true, hadn't you?"

"I guess so," Tiffany said, "ever since Granny Smith gave me that book. And when she died, I did ask. I didn't believe in them, but I wanted to believe because she believed."

"They answered you," Josh said with a smile. "They always answer anyone who asks. But if you aren't really looking, you miss them. You can see what's going on, you can see others with Spirit Flyers, but you don't notice or don't understand. But when you bow to the Kingson, then it's like your eyes are opened and you can see, at last."

"That's the problem, isn't it?" Tiffany said. "Bowing down before him. That was the hardest part, at least at first. That's what will be hard for Sloan. He doesn't want to bow down to anybody but himself. I'm afraid he won't choose to be a part of his kingdom if he has to bow down."

"The kings don't force anyone to bow," Josh said with a shrug. "But they're in charge. I trust them to know what they're doing."

"Me too," Tiffany said firmly. "No matter what else happens, I'm going to trust them too. I mean, if you can't trust him, whom can you trust?"

"He's the best, that's for sure," Josh said.

"I just hope Sloan and my family will trust him too," Tiffany said. "Boy, are they going to be surprised when I tell them the news. They won't believe I have this bike!"

Tiffany laughed out loud, high up above the countryside. The two riders talked and rode, and even circled around the town of Centerville a few extra times so they could talk some more and look at the lights below.

Tiffany felt like she could talk and ride all night, even when she and Josh landed on Buckingham Street.

NEUTRALIZED
· · · · · · · · · · ·
18

Tiffany had never felt so wonderful and alive as she did when she woke up the next morning. She jumped out of bed, got dressed, and ran downstairs and burst into the kitchen.

"You won't guess what happened," Tiffany announced excitedly. Mr. and Mrs. Favor were drinking coffee at the table. Mr. Favor was reading a newspaper. Mrs. Favor was spreading margarine on a sweet roll.

"I met the Prince of Kings last night," Tiffany said.

"What?" Mrs. Favor asked. She put down the butter knife.

"Last night, Sloan and I went on a mission for extra credit so we could get the parts in the movie," Tiffany said. "But it was all a big trick. They were really just trying to hurt the people out at the Kramar farm. But the Kingson came and I met him. I even danced with him. And he gave me a Spirit Flyer."

"What?" Mrs. Favor said. Her mother looked totally puzzled. "What on earth are you talking about?"

"I'm telling you," Tiffany said impatiently. "Sloan can tell you too. By the way, where is Sloan?"

"I don't know," Mrs. Favor said. "He went out early this morning. What did you say about the Kramar farm and them trying to trick you?"

"No, it was the other way around," Tiffany said. "Sloan and I were going to put some chemical in their water, but before we could—"

"What did you say about putting chemicals in water?" Mr. Favor asked. He put down his newspaper and looked at Tiffany.

Just then, the doorbell rang. Mr. Favor frowned and got up. Tiffany heard him talking at the front door. When he returned, he was followed by a whole crowd of people. Dr. Burke led the way, followed by Grandfather Kramar, Bill Kramar, Josh Smedlowe, Mr. Turner the newspaper editor, John and Susan Kramar, Daniel Bayley and Amy Burke.

Mr. Favor led everyone into the large living room, where they sat down. Dr. Burke had a file folder filled with papers and photographs.

"Like I say, I hate to bother you so early in the morning, but the tests are positively conclusive," Dr. Burke said. "I couldn't believe my eyes. I just couldn't. But the evidence is locked away in the safe in my office. Those fire extinguishers were filled with Nega Flu. I wouldn't have known what it was except that we examined those residents from the Glory Road Retirement Home. The Goliath and ORDER companies have been very restrictive about who has had access to what the Nega Flu actually looks like under the microscope. And now I know why. Every ingredient in the Nega Flu is made from chemicals made by Goliath Industries. There's a Traginite-Z base, with Pharmakeia which makes it spread so quickly. But then it's gone suddenly. It doesn't have a long life span. The heck of the thing is that we are the only plant I know producing this kind of Traginite-Z. I've always questioned its valid medical use. And this is just pure . . . murder, I think. This Nega Flu plague appears to be totally synthetic and totally man-made and easily preventable with a simple antidote."

"You mean our little Centerville factory is responsible for helping produce one of the most deadly plagues in modern history?" Mr. Favor asked.

"I'm afraid it is," Dr. Burke said. "They fooled us all. I wondered where all that Traginite-Z was being used. I had suspicions, but I didn't want to believe it. I was too scared. I wanted to keep my job, keep the peace."

"You took fire extinguishers out to the Kramar farm last night?" Mr. Favor asked his daughter in disbelief. His face grew red.

"Yes, I've been trying to tell you, Daddy," Tiffany said. "Both Sloan and I went out there. Mr. Cutright and Professor Pickie sent us."

"But you . . . you could have been killed," Mr. Favor said. "And you would have killed everyone out at the farm."

"Everyone who drank the water," Dr. Burke said. "It doesn't hit right away. It would have taken a few hours since it was diluted. That way, everyone out there probably would have been exposed before they knew what was happening. That little dog died so quickly because he got such a concentrated dose. It's odorless and tasteless and colorless. But the eerie thing is this. It doesn't last long. It disappears soon without a trace. That's why it's been so hard to find how it's spread. All that's left is the bodies. And even in the bodies, it soon disappears."

The room was silent. Mr. Turner was writing quickly on his tablet. Mrs. Favor put her hand over her mouth.

"Where's Sloan?" Mr. Favor asked.

"He ran out of here this morning," Mrs. Favor said. "He said he had to do some kind of errand for Professor Pickie to get the role in the movie."

"But he was all right?" Mr. Favor asked.

"He seemed like himself, just in a hurry," Mrs. Favor said.

"I want to go out to the factory with you, Dr. Burke," Mr. Favor said seriously. "I want you to come too, Mr. Turner."

"I told you Goliath and ORDER were up to no good," Josh said. "We've had reports from other independent newspaper reporters and editors about this Nega Flu in other places, not just overseas, but in this country. In each case, the people who got infected were older people, like in the Glory Road Retirement Home, or people with Spirit Flyer bicycles. But everyone is scared to report it or talk about it."

"This is disturbing news," Mr. Favor said. "But surely Mr. Cutright and Professor Pickie are acting on their own. I still can't believe what they did would be the official policy of ORDER or Goliath."

"Mr. Favor, you and I both know how odd Mr. Cutright has acted at times," Dr. Burke said. "And we've both heard him talk about plans to get rid of people that are seen as enemies of the government, like the people who didn't want to take number cards. I thought it was idle talk at first, but now I realize that he meant every word."

"And I heard him talking to Professor Pickie," Tiffany said. "I couldn't really believe they were trying to do something that awful."

"What did you hear?" Mr. Favor asked. Tiffany quickly told them how she had gone down to the warehouse. As she told her story, everyone listened in silence.

"I just didn't understand it all," Tiffany said. "Or maybe I didn't want to believe it either. I thought Professor Pickie was a good person."

"We've been tricked," Mr. Favor said. "I would have never believed it. Their real aim is to experiment with the Nega Flu and their vaccine as they Number Mark people. They intend to exterminate anyone who's not Number Marked and doesn't have the vaccine. How could I have been so stupid?"

"We all wanted to believe the best," Dr. Burke said. "I know I did. Still, we have the evidence. We have proof now. We must expose this . . . this terrible scheme."

"We've got to destroy those chemicals before they do more harm," Mr. Favor said with new determination.

"But there's thousands of gallons," Dr. Burke said. "I don't know how we'd get rid of it. You can't just dump it out on the ground; the environmental pollution would be disastrous."

Mr. Favor looked perplexed. He shook his head. Dr. Burke stood beside him.

"There must be a way to destroy it all."

Dr. Burke nodded. He looked worried. His forehead was covered in sweat. His eyes brightened.

"I know a way we could neutralize it," Dr. Burke said. "That would almost be as good as destroying it. Only there might be a lot of pressure from the excess gases."

"That's right!" Mr. Favor said. "You could dilute the formula of the Traginite-Z. Quality control has always been a problem, but if we ran Dikaiosune into it, that would work."

"What's that?" Mr. Kramar asked.

"Traginite-Z looks very much like Dikaiosune, with some slight molecular variations," Dr. Burke said. "We've always had a problem with quality control to keep the formula steady. If we added lots of Dikaiosune, it would act as a neutralizing agent for sure. The only trouble is that it might put a lot of pressure on the tanks and lines."

"We'll have to risk it," Mr. Favor said. "It's our best chance of stalling this thing. Then maybe if we appealed to headquarters, they would reconsider. I want you to get on the loudspeaker system and call all the workers together in the cafeteria."

Everyone rode out to the Goliath factory in a hurry. Mr. Favor rode in his car, but Tiffany and the others rode on their Spirit Flyers. The old red bicycles refused to be parked outside, but rolled down the halls to the cafeteria. Within a few minutes, bells were ringing and buzzers sounded as all the workers at the Goliath factory stopped doing their jobs. Everyone knew there was an emergency of some sort.

"All personnel report immediately to the cafeteria for an emergency meeting," Mr. Favor announced.

Soon the cafeteria was filled with curious workers. Mr. Favor stood up and explained in detail what had been going on. The workers looked surprised at first and then angry.

"I don't think we have any other choice but to neutralize these tanks of . . . poison, and appeal to the government to reconsider these policies," Mr. Favor said. "Dr. Burke knows a simple way we can do this, though this may create pressure in the tanks and lines. What I need to know, is are you with us?"

"Yes," the voices shouted out. Every face looked determined.

"Just one minute!" a man shouted out. Every head turned. At the back of the room, Cyrus Cutright stood in the doorway holding a megaphone with two Security Squad guards behind him. They were holding guns.

"If any one of you tries to carry out this treasonous plan, you will be stopped, one way or the other," Mr. Cutright said, spitting out the words. His face was filled with fury. "How dare you even think of destroying Goliath property? Every ounce of every chemical we've made in here has been sold to the government already under contract. If you destroy it, you'll also be destroying property belonging to ORDER. I want all of you back on your jobs. The Number Marking and vaccination plan will go on tomorrow as planned. Do I make myself clear?"

The workers paused. The air was tense. Then Josh turned on the light of his Spirit Flyer, aiming it at the old man. The others turned on their lights too. Mr. Cutright howled as if scorched by fire. Everyone gasped when they saw deeper through the light. A large black snake, shaped like a cobra, seemed to be attached to Mr. Cutright's back. Its great hooded head overshadowed Mr. Cutright. The eyes of the serpent glowed red. In the beams of light, whirls of smoke began to rise off his body, as if he were being burned.

"Back to work!" Mr. Cutright said, only this time, the voice was coming out of the moving mouth of the serpent. The mouths of the two

guards dropped open in surprised horror.

"Kill them all, you fools," the serpent's head hissed loudly to the security guards. They looked at the snake and then back at the roomful of workers. "Do it now!"

The Security Guards looked at each other and together turned so their guns pointed straight at Mr. Cutright. The workers let out a shout and cheer.

Mr. Cutright hissed, fell to the floor and slid backward out the door in great puffs of black smoke. The lights of the Spirit Flyers cleared the air.

The workers yelled and cheered as Mr. Cutright retreated. Mr. Favor stood in front of the microphone.

"I want all of you to leave the factory except those Dr. Burke and I announce," Mr. Favor said. "This is for your own safety since we're not exactly sure how the Traginite-Z will respond to the neutralizing agent. I think it's best that I accompany the Security Guards over to the Security Center across the street to explain what's going on."

Dr. Burke stood up and announced a list of names. The workers moved quickly. The two Security Guards also left with Mr. Favor.

Dr. Burke stood near a large tank. He checked a page on his clipboard and began turning the large valve on a pipe. A bubbling and gurgling sound could be heard as the Dikaiosune ran into the big tank. Hissing steam rose up in great fury as the two chemicals searched for balance. Watching a needle move up on a meter, Dr. Burke opened the pipe wider to overpower the Traginite-Z.

A few hours later, Mr. Favor came through the front door of his house. He looked excited and happy, yet tired. Dr. Burke and Mr. Smedlowe and Josh were with him.

"We did it!" Mr. Favor told his wife and children. "We actually did it. Everyone has agreed. The whole town has turned against this ORDER plan."

"You're kidding!" Sloan said. "How could you? We'll be ruined for life! We'll never live this down."

"There's a time when a person has to make a stand," Mr. Favor said. He looked at Josh with admiration. "I've called the Goliath headquarters in the capital."

"Are you fired?" Sloan asked with a moan.

"No, they just listened," Mr. Favor said. "I explained that Cutright and this Professor Pickie had gone mad. They said they would look into it right away. They told us not to say anything to anyone until they had time to investigate."

"Everything out at the plant has been neutralized," Dr. Burke said.

"The best part was all the guys at the Security Center," Josh said. "Everyone of them except that Nazi Captain Sharp has resigned. He was running around screaming. When they turned their guns on him, he shut up quick enough. The last we saw of him, he was picked up on the road by Professor Pickie's big white limousine. We saw Cutright in there with him. They all headed out of town."

"I hope we never see them again," Dr. Burke said. "But I imagine they'll be back to defend themselves."

"We'll be ready," Mr. Favor said. "I've talked to Mr. Turner, and the newspaper is going to print the whole story in a late edition to be circulated today. Instead of going through this Number Marking business, we plan to sign a petition and send it to the government. Then we plan to go down there together and protest. I'll call some of my old colleagues once the phone lines are working again. The ones I've talked to so far say they've been having a lot of second thoughts about ORDER policies too."

Sloan listened in silence. His hands were clenched in fists. He ran out of the house and jumped on his Goliath Super Wings. In moments he was gone.

CELEBRATING
FREEDOM
• • • • • • • •
19

On July Fourth, Tiffany rode her old red bicycle down the driveway. Across the street, Josh waved excitedly from the Smedlowe house. He jumped onto his Spirit Flyer and crossed over.

"I've got great news!" Josh said.

"What?" Tiffany asked.

"My parents are here," Josh said. "They arrived last night. I thought for sure they were goners. But they've been working back east, writing and investigating ORDER's activities and plans. We told them about what had happened here and the Nega Flu. They say they've heard several reports of small towns in this country where the same kind of thing has been happening. They think ORDER chose Centerville to be one of those experimental towns. But Centerville's especially important because of the factory here."

"It's wonderful that you get to be with them again," Tiffany said, smiling. "They're here just in time for the parade."

"I know," Josh said. "Can you believe how fast things have changed in Centerville? Once the Goliath factory shut down, the Kingson just came in. Everyone in town has seen him, it seems."

"All my friends and their families have Spirit Flyers," Tiffany said. "Everyone but Sloan."

"Your parents still don't know where he is?" Josh asked with concern.

"No one has seen him since he left the house," Tiffany said. "We all went out looking for him last night. We looked all over town and then flew over the countryside around here."

"He'll show up sooner or later," Josh said. "Maybe he's just scared to see all the Spirit Flyers. Everyone in town has them."

"And they're all gathering for the parade," Tiffany said. "We better get over there. I wouldn't miss this for anything."

The south end of Main Street was packed with people. Tiffany and Josh rode over. Everywhere they looked, kids and adults were on Spirit Flyer bicycles. Amy, Daniel and Barry were all there with their parents. Susan Kramar and her sisters were riding with her dad and mom, who carried six-month-old Paul Nathaniel in a backpack. Right next to them was John Kramar. His mom and dad rode along too. They looked so much stronger and healthier than even just a couple of months ago.

Joe Kramar rode his bicycle in a loop up in the air, even flying upside down for a few seconds. Everyone laughed and clapped. Soon others were flying in loops and circles and zigzags above the street. Mr. Peek and Mr. Penn, the two attorneys-at-law, were flying and laughing because they weren't holding onto the handlebars with their hands. Their bright red suspenders matched the red color of the old bicycles. Everyone was having a good time in Centerville. The parade was about to begin.

The sun was shining brightly. And the star hanging in the sky also seemed brighter and more glorious than ever, Tiffany thought.

"I hope he likes the parade," she said to herself. The school marching band was assembled and practicing their warm-up notes. Some were hastily getting into formation. Then there was a moment of quiet as Mr. Martini, the conductor, got the band's attention. He waved his baton and the music began.

Grandfather Kramar's big red tractor, the Spirit Flyer Harvester, was at the front of the parade. His wife and Aunt Thelma Kramar sat on the big wheel covers as the tractor chugged down the street. Almost everyone rode a Spirit Flyer, except those in the band. After all, it was just too hard to play a tuba and ride a bike, even if it was a bike as special as a Spirit Flyer. The whole town was out, either watching or marching or flying overhead, playing flight tag on the Spirit Flyers.

The band played old songs and new songs, marches and hymns. Everywhere you looked, people were celebrating freedom. Not only were they free from the troubles with ORDER, but more important, they were free from their chains.

On the last block on Main Street, just south of the town square, everyone gathered together in a group. The whole street was jammed with bicycles and people. With Grandfather Kramar leading the way, they began to sing about the kings and the wonders of the Kingson himself. They were still singing as they flooded into the town square, packing it solid. There were so many people on the ground that several children and adults flew their bicycles up and landed on top of the buildings in the square so they could get a better view.

While everyone was singing, the giant Big Board hanging on the courthouse began to smoke and spark and sputter. Everyone cheered and sang louder. As they sang, they all aimed their Spirit Flyers toward the courthouse. At Grandfather Kramar's signal, they turned on their lights.

In a flash and a crack, the giant Big Board sizzled and exploded into a zillion tiny fireballs that shot out over the square like big fireworks. The little balls of fire burned up into puffs of smoke. For a moment, everyone was silent. Then the whole town square exploded into cheers and laughter and song.

With the lights still aimed at the courthouse, a loud hissing noise rumbled through the square. The ground shook, and the dome of the courthouse seemed to be breaking apart. The people sang louder about the wonder of the kings and the greatness and glory of the Kingson. As they sang their loudest, a giant shadow rose up out of the courthouse roof. No one seemed surprised to see the giant black serpent writhing and twisting, trying to escape. His head was as big as the courthouse dome. As they aimed their lights on the shadowy snake, it hissed even louder, its great body jerking in pain.

Suddenly, everyone assembled could see them. All around the serpent, dressed in shining white clothes, they moved closer to the struggling form. In the midst of the singing from the town square, they drove the serpent up out of the courthouse. With drawn swords, hundreds of them followed him into the sky. The great snake twisted more and more frantically as it left its den.

"Who are those guys?" Tiffany asked staring in awe.

"Those are the Aggeloi," Josh said.

"They're on our side, right?"

"Of course they are," Josh said with a smile. "They're sort of like the kings' army. At least the invisible part. But every once in a while you'll see them."

"I'm just glad they're friendly," Tiffany said. Watching them almost made her afraid.

When the tail of the giant serpent left the top of the courthouse, the whole town of Centerville broke into a shout and cheer. And when they did, the Aggeloi rushed forward with their swords. In a shrieking hiss, the giant serpent began to break apart into thousands of wiggling black baby snakes that scattered and then disappeared in puffs of heavy, dark smoke. Down below, the crowd cheered again as they watched the snakes disintegrate.

"Wow!" Tiffany whispered. "Did you see that?"

"Everyone in town saw that," Josh said and laughed.

Grandfather Kramar climbed up the courthouse steps. He stood in front of the waiting microphone.

"The victory we've just witnessed belongs to the Prince of Kings," the old man said. Everyone clapped. "By him, all things are made. And because of him, we are free today, not only from our enemies, but more important, free from our own chains."

The people shouted and cheered again. Tiffany whooped and hollered so loud she felt embarrassed for an instant. But then she realized that given what she was feeling, it was perfectly natural to be making a loud noise.

"Today we praise the Prince of Kings, and give thanks for our freedom," the old man said. "We know that no matter what happens in the future, the Prince of Kings is on his throne, and that soon he is returning to claim everything that belongs to his kingdom."

A deep quiet filled the town square. Everyone looked up at the star hanging in the noonday sky. Tears filled Tiffany's eyes, but she wasn't sure why. For a moment, she thought she could see him.

"I know we're all here to honor our king," Grandfather Kramar said. "And I know of no better honor to him than to celebrate the freedom he's given us all. So let's begin the party!"

Everyone cheered again. The people began to dance in the square. The air was filled with flying bicycles playing flight tag and other games. The whole town was celebrating and having fun. Tiffany began pedaling her Spirit Flyer up into the sky. The air was thick with old red bicycles. She laughed when she saw an old red tractor rise up into the air and circle the roof of the courthouse.

The beautiful music filled the air. Everyone was so busy laughing and playing and talking and singing that they didn't even notice the planes coming toward the town. The planes flew just below the clouds. A white circle with an X inside was painted on the side of each plane. There seemed to be thirty or more, all lined up evenly across the sky. Their engines droned and got louder as they came closer.

The whole town was still celebrating when the planes arrived. Great black smoke began billowing out of the planes like a heavy fog. The line of fog grew like a great black blanket.

"What's that?" Tiffany said to Josh. She coughed once.

But the planes were overhead now, and the blanket of fog was rapidly falling like a mist. In a instant, the whole town of Centerville froze. The music stopped. The bicycles hovered in midair. Every person in town seemed to be frozen like a statue. The planes moved on.

Before they were out of sight, Tiffany shook her head, as if she were waking up. In a twinkling, every eye was opened. For a moment, everyone was quiet. Then they saw them. For miles and miles around the town, there was a circle of the men in shining clothes. Thousands upon thousands of them. They came closer, and they were singing.

"Look at all of them," Tiffany said to Josh. "They're coming for us, aren't they?"

"They're the host of the kings," Josh said in awe. "I've never seen so many."

Then they saw him in the distance. Sitting on a glorious white throne in the midst of the hosts of Aggeloi was the Prince of Kings himself. Tiffany looked around. All the people in Centerville were rising up, moving toward the Prince. His arms were open wide, and he was smiling.

"We're going to live with him now, aren't we?" Tiffany said with a smile. "We're going to be with him forever. I can just feel it."

Josh smiled and looked around. Centerville already seemed far, far away below them, almost like a place in a dream.

"I wasn't sure what it would be like," Josh said. He rode over near his family. His father hugged him.

Tiffany found herself next to her family. Her father's eyes were wet as he stared at the Prince of Kings. Her mother's eyes were wet too. Tiffany looked around, hoping to see Sloan, but her brother wasn't there.

IT'S SAFE NOW

· · · · · · · · ·

20

Out at the Goliath factory, Cyrus Cutright chewed bitterly on a short, used cigar. His eyes glowed red as he looked out the window and saw all the bicycles flying overhead. He was in his office with Captain Sharp, Professor Pickie, an old woman named Mrs. Happy and a man in a black derby named Horace Grinsby. They all stared in disbelief at the sky filled with soaring red bicycles.

"This is your fault!" he hissed at Captain Sharp and Professor Pickie. " 'Give them extra credit,' you said. 'Make them sweat it out. Make them suffer.' "

"You ate just as many ashes on their suffering as we did, if not more," Captain Sharp spat out.

"Yeah, and you're the one who let Favor get out of hand," Professor Pickie said. "After all, you were the factory president. I'd hate to be around when headquarters deals with you."

"Oh, shut up, you fool," Cutright said, as he bit his cigar clean in two. He chewed up the portion in his mouth slowly. "You and your movie! You just had to bring in those bratty kids and push them too far."

"It worked with the Favor boy," Pickie said. "He's on line now, all the way. He bought the whole plan."

"Who cares about one boy in a whole town that's turned against us?"

"It was that Kramar boy who was the first target," Pickie said. "If Grinsby had taken him out and his family, like he was supposed to, none of this would have happened."

"It was this old hag's fault," said Grinsby, pointing at Mrs. Happy. "She had them all eating out of the palm of her hand in the toy store. Then she let them get away!"

"It was Grinsby's fault all right," the old woman said. "If Grinsby had done his job, I could have done mine. But, of course, he couldn't X-remove a dead flea."

"You're all to blame," said Captain Sharp. "If you two and that stupid clown, Uncle Bunkie, hadn't messed up on your assignments, I could have had this town under total control by now. But no, you bumblers just fanned the flames of their rebellion. I know my team did their part."

"Your people all ran like chickens as soon as that Favor started opening his big mouth," Cutright said to Captain Sharp. "You assured me that they were loyal, that they were prepared for any emergency, but Mr. Favor yells help and all the men in your command just roll over and join his side, rebels every one."

"But you saw the power they displayed," Captain Sharp said, his eyes glowing red. "I told headquarters we needed backup. I told them there was a cloud brewing here of unprecedented size for this little town. We were outnumbered by their flame throwers. How did we know how much help they would get? All our communication has been jammed since April."

"Excuses, excuses, all of you," Professor Pickie said. "I know I'm not taking the rap for this thing. I came prepared. This wasn't my town. You assured me things were ripe. Well, they were ripe, ripe for rebellion and upset. Now I've got negative points on my perfect record for the first time ever."

"Perfect record, you sun-tanned gila monster," Cutright said, popping the other piece of cigar into his mouth. His eyes glowed so red that it seemed like flames were beginning to show. "I ought take your pretty boy looks and record and throw it right in—"

Cutright stopped. Everyone turned and looked down the hall. There they were, standing quietly, filling the place. They held flaming swords and their eyes blazed too, with a different light, a steady light that made the others squint and cover their faces. The Aggeloi raised their swords.

"We're going! We're going!" Cutright screamed. "See what you let in here! How dare they come right into this factory! See how far it's gone. They're taking over. On the UltraFlights, quick!"

They rushed for the black bicycles. As vials of Wildbird Drops were sucked into the TRAG units, they were already pedaling. The bicycles wobbled and shook and jerked as they rose into the air and went out the window. The Aggeloi came closer, and the UltraFlights crashed in a heap of spokes and sprockets and spinning flat tires. Cutright was the first to be up and running. The others were close behind.

All the way out the factory gates and down Cemetery Road they all ran, the Aggeloi close behind them. Cutright turned and shook his fist.

"We'll get you, you'll see," he screamed. "You can't get away with this!"

At his words, an Aggeloi blew, and the wind of his breath burned away the remaining thin hair of the old man so he became bald in an instant. The others, seeing Mr. Cutright's new haircut, screamed and began running again, this time afraid to look back. The Aggeloi followed, their

voices ringing with praise and laughter at the sight of the running fug-
itives from light.

As the Aggeloi continued to chase them away from town, the planes
passed over and the fog settled.

Sloan Favor was sitting on a pile of garbage out at the dump when
he saw the planes coming in the distance. He stood up and whooped.

"All right! The cavalry is finally coming," he yelled to no one. "They'll
get things back in ORDER."

The planes passed over, and the black fog began to cover the town.
Sloan stared at it fearfully. As the mist came down over the dump, the
boy coughed a few times, but then he felt fine. He ran over to a small
shack that he had built and slept in. He got his Super Wings bike and
began to pedal down the old dump road.

Sloan crossed the bridge over the Sleepy Eye River and rode onto
Crofts Road. He pedaled for town.

His bike began to wobble and shake as he passed into the city limits.
He cursed when he saw that both tires had gone flat. He stopped and
threw the bike down in disgust and started running.

He stopped at his house, but nobody was home. In fact, the town
seemed amazingly quiet. He ran back outside, but there was no one on
the street.

"Where is everyone?" Sloan yelled. Then he ran down Buckingham
and headed for the town square.

He ran up Main Street. Everything was empty, as if Centerville was a
ghost town. The quiet made the boy feel creepy.

Then he saw them, all up ahead in the town square. Sloan ran faster
past the stores and shops. As he burst into the square, he stopped,
staring. He found the people, all right. The whole square was filled with
them—hundreds of people, all frozen like statues.

"Hey, what's going on?" Sloan asked to himself quietly. Then he
started saying it louder and louder to several statues he passed. "What's

going on?" But no one spoke. He ran over and pushed down a boy holding a trumpet. The boy was smiling as he looked up into the sky. Sloan looked up at the sky. He could still see traces of the dark foggy mist that had fallen from the planes.

Sloan ran from body to body, but they were all the same. "Wake up!" he cried. "Hey, wake up!" Everyone was smiling and seemed happy, but no one moved. No one answered. Frantically Sloan ran up the steps into the courthouse. But it was empty. The Number Marking box was lying in a million pieces on the floor, as if someone had blown it up with dynamite. The cold empty silence made him feel more and more uneasy. He ran back outside to the sunshine in the square.

"Mom! Dad!" he screamed. Then he saw them. He ran down to where they were standing, frozen. "Dad, I'm back. Mom, do you hear me?" They stood smiling, saying nothing. "Mom, Dad, listen to me!" he insisted. He shook them. There was no answer.

Then Sloan stopped. The color left his face. His hands grew cold. He felt as though he were the only star on a movie set, only he wasn't acting. This was for real, even if it did seem like a horror film.

"I have the antidote, so it didn't get me," Sloan said softly to himself. "It didn't get me," he repeated numbly.

"Hey, somebody answer me!" he suddenly started shouting again. "I asked them to send the planes so we would win. And we won! Come on out. It's safe now! I saved us all."

The Centerville town square looked extremely peaceful and quiet, all except for a boy running and shouting.

THE
GREAT
FEAST
· · · · · · · ·
21

In another place, not so far from Center-
ville, a party was about to begin. Tiffany and her family moved closer
and closer to the Prince of Kings, seated on his white throne. But as they
got closer, it seemed as if there was a huge wall of window glass between them and the prince on his throne. The glass was clear and
sparkled as if it was made of diamond. As all the people approached
the throne, it appeared that they would have to pass through this glass
before going to the Prince.

"What is that?" Tiffany asked her father.

"I'm not sure," he said. "But I think we have to go through it."

And he was right. All around them, people began stepping into the sparkling glass. As Tiffany got closer, she realized it wasn't made of diamond at all, but of fire! The whole wall or window was burning so hot that it was clear and barely shimmering. But everyone was stepping into it. Tiffany didn't feel afraid exactly, but she did feel uncertain. Still, there was no question that she would go through it like everyone else.

On her right, she saw Granny Smith. She smiled at Tiffany.

"Everything will be just fine," Granny Smith said. Tiffany smiled back. Granny Smith stepped into the glass and disappeared.

Tiffany stepped forward too. For a moment she thought she sensed heat. Everything seemed to be on fire and burning. And in that moment she turned and looked back. Everything was as clear as a movie. She could see her whole life and even the lives of many others she had known. She saw pain and anguish and deceit, and it was all burning away. The diamond fire kept burning and burning, until Tiffany thought nothing would remain in her life. But there were parts of her life that seemed golden and good and did remain. The fire only made the girl more grateful for those rich gifts of life that she had experienced. Soon those were all that was left, the golden rich gifts of life.

Tiffany looked from that window and found that she could see Centerville and even the world. She watched history unfold before her eyes. It was as if she could see anywhere and everywhere she wanted. Some of what she saw made her sad as she thought about those she had left, like Sloan, who were living out their lives in time. She felt grateful that she had been spared the misery and evil that worked out to its conclusion. All the while, the star came closer and closer until all those left cried out for rescue from the paths they had chosen.

The sky burned up like a sheet as the star passed by. Mountains melted and the seas boiled dry, and then it was over. Tiffany took a deep breath and walked out of the burning window. In her hands, she carried those golden gifts that had remained through the fire. She immediately felt clean and pure in a way she couldn't describe. It was as if she had taken a bath in water made of glory, and all the glory had filled her.

Then she turned and saw who had washed her with the glorious water of life. The Kingson sat on his throne and watched as all his children came through the burning glass clean and pure and full of life, carrying their gifts. Some had more gifts than others, but each held something. Tiffany took a step toward him and felt as if she were being born into a new life and dimension. She carried her golden gifts.

"Wow!" was all she could say. Her parents and friends surrounding her were all saying the same sort of thing. They were filled with quiet awe and wonder as they looked on him. Tiffany noticed her body. She felt like both a girl and an adult at the same time. But the important thing was that she knew she was his child and in his family. All the others around her, even her own parents, were like brothers and sisters. Everyone was family and had always been her family, she realized, because they all belonged to him.

Tiffany moved closer. As she came to his throne, she bowed down and laid her golden gifts at his feet. He smiled. All the others, too, laid their gifts down at his feet.

Tiffany looked up. As soon as she looked into his eyes, she realized how much he knew her and loved her. And in that instant, a new, even more beautiful sense of peace filled. her. She felt complete and whole because she was known by the one who knew everything. Then she understood that now she would know as she was known, that all her questions would be answered, and that she had her place in life and in the lives of everyone around her. Such knowledge and acceptance blew through her like music on the wind. She breathed deeply of the gift that he was giving so it filled her heart. For the first time, Tiffany knew that before she had only been tasting life, but now she was filled with his life. She laughed out loud.

As she stood up, laughing, Tiffany realized she was in the great feast hall in the king's palace. The huge table was set. Everyone was taking a seat. Tiffany sat down in the midst of her family. The feast was about to begin.